CRUEL EDGE

"You're going to die, kid," the half-breed announced harshly.

Kirkby swallowed hard. But not all the saliva in his mouth. Some spilled out over his trembling lower lip and ran down his chin. "I know it," he croaked.

"Confession is good for the soul." Edge stepped up close to the injured youngster and gripped the lapels of the open topcoat with his left hand while his right pressed the muzzle of the Remington tight against the pulsing temple.

"What else can you do to me, mister?" Kirkby said, and managed to get a note of defiance into his voice.

"Make it quick. Like you were a horse with no hope. Feller can take a long time to die with a bullet in his belly."

Up close—over a range of no more than six inches—the lean face did not look so evil to the dying man. It was devoid of all emotion, good or bad. Kirkby sucked in a deep breath to power out words without pauses between them. "Please, mister! I don't wanna die! I told you what you wanted!"

"Obliged, kid." Edge clicked back the hammer of the revolver.

D0778342

THE EDGE SERIES:

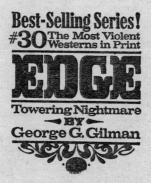

Best-Selling Series!

#30 The Most Violent Westerns in Print

EDGE

Towering Nightmare

BY

George G. Gilman

PINNACLE BOOKS • LOS ANGELES

EDGE #30: TOWERING NIGHTMARE

First American edition.
First published in Great Britain by New English Library Limited, 1979.

A Pinnacle Books edition, published by special arrangement with New English Library, London.

First printing, June 1979

ISBN: 0-523-40531-6

Cover illustration by Bruce Minney

Printed in the United States of America

PINNACLE BOOKS, INC.
2029 Century Park East
Los Angeles, California 90067

TOWERING NIGHTMARE

Chapter One

As HE stood in the luxuriously appointed barroom of the Fifth Avenue Hotel sipping high-priced bourbon and contemplating the pleasant prospect of a train ride into the far west, it would have been easy for the man called Edge to think of himself as one of the sights of New York City. For, as was his nature, he was constantly alert to everything that was happening around him even though he appeared to be totally concerned with his private thoughts.

He was aware of the ebb and flow of well-dressed patrons and the smoothly efficient bartenders in matching shirts and string ties who served drinks with smiles and then seemed to regret the need to accept payment.

The men behind the polished bar eyed Edge with surreptitious suspicion whenever they were between orders and thought he was not looking at them. The customers—whether men or women—were variously intrigued, curious, shocked, disgusted and perturbed to see this obvious interloper in their midst.

It was his clothing which first caught the attention of the native New Yorkers and visitors to the city who had chosen to conform with local custom. For here, in one of the most sophisticated establishments on the eastern seaboard of the United States, Edge was dressed western-style. A gray, low-crowned, wide-brimmed Stetson, a black leather jacket, gray shirt, black denim

1

pants and black riding boots without spurs. Around his waist was slung a gunbelt with a Remington revolver in the holster, one side of his unbuttoned jacket pulled back to both display and allow him easy access to the gun. A gray kerchief was tied loosely at his throat, not quite concealing a beaded thong that hugged the flesh more tightly just below his Adam's apple.

Not only was the style and cut of the clothing completely out of place in the smart barroom of an ostentatious New York hotel, its condition also left much to be desired. For it showed many signs of age and hard wear—was shiny and scuffed, torn and stained. So that perhaps all that could be said for the man's outfit in such splendid surroundings was that at least it had been brushed free of trail dust.

The man who wore the clothing also displayed many signs of age and hard wear and everyone who happened to be caught in the act of surveying the incongruous westerner felt compelled to look hurriedly away and be more cautious if they glanced again in his direction.

Edge had this effect on strangers without any need to make an effort. This was in part due to the accidents of his build and the formation of his features and the rest was contributed by the experiences of the recent past, his stature and face presenting a forbidding aspect.

He was a tall man who stood more than six feet three inches in his riding boots and he had a firm-fleshed physique which gave him a weight in the region of two hundred pounds, the bulk evenly distributed to suggest a deceptive leanness. This impression was augmented by the cut and set of his features which were drawn from the dual nationalities of his parents—a Mexican father and a Scandinavian mother. It was a long face, the skin stained dark by heritage and exposure to the extremes of weather and stretched taut between the high cheekbones and firm jawline. There was a hawk-like quality in the set of the nose and more than a mere hint of latent cruelty in the width and narrowness of the mouth. But it was the eyes of the man which revealed the greatest clue to his character. Permanently narrowed under their hooded lids they were of the palest blue color and totally devoid of expression, unmistakably piercing in the manner they surveyed the world and yet looking like no more than slivers of ice chipped from a frozen ocean.

The stretched, dark skin was engraved by countless lines splaying from the corners of the eyes and mouth and the face was framed by thick-growing, jet black hair that reached to the shoulders of the man. Recently washed up and shaved—something else the patrons and bartenders were prepared to allow in his favor—he sported an unobtrusive mustache that followed the line of his top lip and curved down at each side of his mouth.

Anyone who had the inclination and opportunity to look closely at him might well judge his age correctly to be in the late thirties, but on first impression he looked several years older than this. Of the women who eyed him, some considered him hauntingly handsome; others were repelled by the strong impression of ugliness they received.

Nobody felt able to ignore him.

"Guess a feller like you knows about horseflesh, sir," a man said.

Like Edge, the short, tubby, balding individual who spoke had entered the barroom alone and not met anybody there. All the other patrons had entered as couples or in groups or had joined friends. In all other respects the man who spoke fitted perfectly into the surroundings. He was well and expensively dressed, city style, and had appeared to be using the place to kill some time before he went out to dinner or to a theatre. He

3

had been standing at the bar when the half-breed entered, half a whiskey ago, and had been showing more than average interest in the tall man with the cold blue eyes; he had needed two shots and most of a beer chaser to bring him fifteen feet along the counter and talk to Edge.

"Don't claim to be an expert."

"But you're from Texas or some place like that, sir?"

"Iowa. Nothing like Texas, feller."

The man, who was about fifty, shrugged his flabby shoulders. "Whatever. You want to earn some easy money?"

The smell of whiskey on the short man's breath almost masked the sweeter aromas of his pomade and after-shave talc.

"Doing what?"

"Looking over a couple of stallions I'm thinking of purchasing, sir. For my lady wife who has this whim to get into stock breeding. See, I grow tobacco down in Carolina and I've got me some spare acreage. Amy would like to run some horses on the pasture and since we got a twenty-fifth wedding anniversary coming up I plan to indulge her. Feller out on Long Island has these two high-priced stallions to sell, but tobacco is my trade. Can tell a stallion from a gelding and a mare, is about all. Saw you standing here. Obvious you're from the west. Thought to ask you if you'd run out to Long Island with me tomorrow and take a look at the animals. Be there and back before noon. Pay you fifty dollars for your advice. Whether I buy or not, of course."

The man, who stood no higher than Edge's shoulder, looked eagerly up into the deeply lined, sparsely fleshed face of the half-breed. Then showed disappointment at the shake of the head he drew.

"Fee's too high for someone who isn't an expert, feller. And anyway, I don't plan to be in New York that

4

long. Be heading out of Grand Central in less than two hours."

The man nodded, still glum. "No harm in asking, was there? You didn't mind me asking, sir?"

"No sweat."

"Buy you a drink?"

"I already got one."

"Drink up and I'll buy you another." He finished his beer with a single swallow and crooked a finger toward one of the bartenders.

"No, thanks. I pay my own way."

The short man seemed about to insist, but then saw at close range the depths of coldness in the narrowed blue eyes and asked the bartender for just one bourbon.

"This is one lousy town, isn't it?" he said after he had paid for the drink. "I have to come here to do business sometimes. Never can wait to get out of it and down south fast enough."

"Guess there are worse places," Edge answered. "Never have been to them, though."

There had been a subtle change of atmosphere in the barroom. A lightening of mood among the patrons and an easing of the tension which had affected the bartenders. Almost as if everyone felt more relaxed now that one of their kind had approached the dangerous-looking stranger without paying any kind of price for his recklessness. Levels of conversations rose above a whisper, there were sincere smiles on some faces and occasionally a burst of laughter sounded. Only the tobacco grower from Carolina—who had caused the uneasiness to evaporate—found himself experiencing a disconcerting anxiety about the tall, taciturn westerner.

"Been here long?"

"No."

"Business trip?"

"Way it started out."

5

It was evident that the man now wanted to detach himself from the half-breed, was doubtless regretting the impulse which had caused him to make the approach. He had run out of openings for conversation and now searched his mind for an excuse to leave.

He gulped down his liquor and said hurriedly, "Well, it's been nice talking to you, sir. Sorry we couldn't do business. Have yourself a good trip back west."

"It has to be better than the trip east," Edge answered, without looking at the tobacco grower as the man set down his empty shot glass on the counter top and swung around, took a first step toward the door which turned out to be his last voluntary action in life.

The report of the gunshot which killed him cut sharply across the sounds of discreet happiness which filled the barroom and instantly silenced them.

Edge dropped his almost empty glass and it hit the counter without breaking, but then rolled and shattered as it fell to the floor. The half-breed had turned by then, in a gunfighter's crouch, the Remington clear of the holster and cocked, muzzle raking across the room toward the point from which the killing shot had been fired. The piercing blue eyes, glinting in the light from the overhead chandeliers, moved ahead of the Remington's barrel on the same arc. To glimpse the shocked face of a young man who stood transfixed in the open doorway of the barroom, seemingly frozen for part of a second in the act of pushing a still smoking Frontier Colt between the lapels of his fastened topcoat. Then the killer, who had blond hair and crooked, widely spaced teeth, made to bring the gun out from his coat again, but realized he had no chance of dropping a man who was only a split second away from drawing a bead on him. So he changed his plan, plunging the Colt into whatever kind of holster he wore under the coat, at the same time as he whirled and lunged to the side, out of the doorway.

The man from Carolina had ceased to twitch by then, had hit the floor under the half-breed's outstretched gun arm, started to roll forward onto his face, bounced against Edge's boots and ankles had been tipped over onto his deck, limbs spread-eagled. Bright red, arterial blood from the wound in the left side of his neck was no longer being spurted out by heartbeats. Instead, it oozed at a rate which slowed with each moment that slipped silently into history in the totally still, shock-filled atmosphere of the barroom. Then every pair of widened eyes shifted their gaze from the doorway to the corpse and then switched between the impassive face of Edge and the Remington fisted in his brown-skinned hand. At the same time as the doorway, which gave on to the spacious lobby of the hotel, became filled with people anxious to see the result of the gunshot.

"I'm the manager!" a man called, shrill and angry and frightened. "I'm the manager! Let me through! Let me through here, please!"

The crowd in the doorway was forced to part to allow entrance into the barroom for a middle-aged, impeccably dressed man who seemed caught between the urge to sob and the need to faint. He came to a sudden halt and stared at the corpse sprawled at the feet of Edge as the half-breed drew back his arm to slide the Remington back into the holster.

The manager covered his gaping mouth with both hands and spoke through his pressed together fingers as Edge straightened up from the half crouch which he had instinctively assumed at the sound of a gunshot.

"Mr. Powell! You've killed Mr. Powell?"

"No, feller," Edge answered.

"He's not dead?" The distraught manager of the hotel experienced a stab of hope.

7

"He's dead all right, Quinn," an evening-dressed customer confirmed in a growling tone. "This guy means he didn't kill him."

"The murderer escaped through the lobby, Mr. Quinn," a woman added. "I saw him."

"So did I."

"Me, too!"

"A kid with yellow hair and . . ."

Quinn held up both hands to silence the babble of voices. "All right, all right, ladies and gentlemen! Please all remain exactly where you are. I'll have the police brought here."

He turned around quickly and this time did not have to fight his way through the crowd in the doorway. They allowed him through without fuss, eager to have an uninterrupted view of the new corpse. With a single exception, everyone complied with Quinn's order to remain seated or standing where they had been at the time of the shooting. The man who ignored the instruction was the one in evening dress who had explained Edge's ambiguous response to the manager's question. He broke away from the group of three similarly attired men with whom he had been drinking and advanced on the corpse—dropped down onto his haunches to look closely at the no longer blood-flowing neck wound. Then, still squatting, he looked up the towering length of the half-breed's frame.

"Something you want, feller?"

The man came erect, almost as tall as Edge but much thinner. About thirty, pasty-faced and tired-eyed with an unruly mop of blond hair.

"Mason Dickens, *New York Daily World*," he introduced. "You know something? If that guy hadn't been stepping around the back of you, the bullet would have got you right between the shoulder blades."

8

Silence had descended on the barroom again, so that the newspaperman's words carried to every ear.

Edge swung toward the bar and looked at the tender closest to him. "Another whiskey, feller. I'll need a fresh glass."

The man gulped. "Certainly, sir."

"I'll buy that," Dickens said, delving a hand into his pants pocket.

But the half-breed was first to place a heap of loose change on the counter top. "I pay my way, feller."

"Suit yourself."

"Usually do."

"You already figured out that shot was meant for you, uh?"

"Sure thing."

"So maybe you know who the killer was?"

"Not yet," Edge answered and swallowed the bourbon as he heard raised voices out in the lobby. He scooped up the change which the bartender had left on the counter and tipped it back into his pocket.

"You're not a very talkative guy, are you?" Dickens muttered, disgruntled as he looked balefully toward the two frock-coated and glazed-capped police patrolmen who entered the barroom ahead of the anxious faced Quinn.

Voices were raised again, as witnesses to the murder competed with each other to give their accounts to the policemen. But the uniformed men were not interested. One of them left to report to his superiors while the other sought to quieten the excited chatter as he closed the doors on the curious bystanders who had not seen the shooting. Under cover of the noise Dickens leaned close to talk fast to Edge.

"Listen, if you mean what I think you do, I can help you. A reporter has to have contacts to do his job. And

9

in a city the size of New York you're going to need help to find the kid with blond hair."

"What do you need, feller?" Edge asked, taking out the makings from his shirt pocket and starting to roll a cigarette.

"A damn good exclusive story that'll make my editor sit up and take notice of me. What do you say?"

"I'm not the talkative type," Edge reminded with a bleak grin.

Dickens showed a fleeting smile that gave his sleepy eyes a more alert look. "Because you're the kind that figures actions speak louder than words?"

The half-breed's mouthline became reset into narrow-lipped cruelty as his face lost all traces of the former grin and he struck a match on the counter front and fired the cigarette. He looked down at the corpse. "Far as I know, nobody ever got talked to death, feller," he muttered. "But I've seen lots like him."

"Like Powell?" Dickens asked as the barroom became quiet again and the patrolman advanced on the half-breed and reporter with the stiffening cadaver at their feet.

Edge nodded. "Killed by a single action."

Chapter Two

THE Captain of Detectives from the local precinct station was named Gilpatrick and he had red hair, green eyes and the kind of demeanor which suggested he would be quick to temper. But there was no hint of an Irish brogue in his voice. He was about fifty with a ruddy complexion. A dead, half-smoked cigar seemed to be a permanent fixture between his thick lips and eyes which viewed everything as if they had seen it all before, countless times.

The half-breed told him what had happened since the Carolina tobacco grower had approached him with the offer of a morning's work, but made no mention of his guess that the blond haired youngster with crooked teeth had hit the wrong target.

"That how you saw it, too, Mase?" Gilpatrick asked when the story was told, acknowledging for the first time that he knew the reporter.

"Sure was, Captain," Dickens confirmed. He glanced around the barroom to indicate the other patrons and the men who tended the bar, many of whom seemed to be trying without success to avoid looking at the corpse which was still sprawled where it had fallen. "And I'd say there's never been a murder in New York with so many eye-witnesses."

"There's never been one here at the hotel," Quinn put in anxiously, using a pure white silk handkerchief to mop sweat beads from his forehead. "It's going to be difficult for us to get over . . ."

Gilpatrick touched the heel of one of Powell's up-turned boots with the toe of his own. "This guy isn't ever going to get over what happened to him, mister."

It was obvious from the way the detective grimaced and spoke that the publicity-sensitive Quinn had already tried to talk Gilpatrick into doing everything possible to play down the killing. Quinn's own expression and tone of voice indicated that he knew full well that he was indulging in wishful thinking. So, submitting to the police captain's authority as an officer of the law, Quinn glowered resentfully at Dickens—a representative of the press which would be the instrument for bringing adverse publicity to the Fifth Avenue Hotel.

The men arrived from the city morgue to remove the body, but Gilpatrick made them wait a few moments while he crouched down to look along an imaginary line between the dead man and the door. Then he stood up, nodded his permission for Powell's remains to be taken away, and ordered the two patrolmen to start taking names, addresses and statements from the rest of the witnesses.

"You from Texas?" he asked Edge, out of the blue.

"Iowa."

"How long you been in New York?"

"Three days."

"Staying here at the hotel?"

"Too rich for my blood and my bank-roll, Captain. Boarding house on Fourth Avenue."

"Why'd you come here this evening, Mr. Edge?"

"A drink is all. Killing some time before my train leaves the Grand Central depot."

"You're a long way from the railroad station, mister."

The half-breed dropped his cigarette to the floor and

12

stepped on it, which drew a scowl from Quinn. "When I got here I had a long while to wait."

"What's the idea, Captain?" Dickens growled. "You're questioning him like you suspect him of something?"

Edge eyed the reporter coldly, aware that his overanxious, protective attitude would serve only to strengthen Gilpatrick's suspicion that Powell had been shot by mistake.

"Go give a patrolman your statement, Mase," the Captain rasped, his green eyes looking almost as hard as the blue ones of the half-breed.

Dickens obviously knew the lawman well enough to recognize the danger signs and he complied without argument, a hangdog expression on his thin face and his skinny shoulders sagging.

Gilpatrick waited until the reporter was out of earshot, then leaned on the counter top and asked for some water. The barman put a few drops in the bottom of a shot glass, knowing from past experience what was required. The detective took a dented silver hip flask from a pocket of his topcoat and poured amber liquid into the glass. It smelled like good brandy.

"You know what I'm getting at, don't you, mister?" he asked, lighting the cigar.

"Powell and me were standing pretty close together when he got it, feller."

A nod as he sipped the brandy and water mix. Then he waved the cigar in the direction of Quinn, who stood a few feet away trying too hard to pretend he was not listening. "Mr. Quinn there said that when he got into the room you had your gun out and were standing like some picture on the front cover of a dime novel."

"Habit, feller. I've been shot at lots of times."

Another nod. "Figured you had. One of them western gunfighters, are you? Lots of that kind of trouble in Iowa?"

"I was born and bred in Iowa, feller. Haven't been back there in a long time. There's trouble all over."

"So I hear, Mr. Edge. We get more than our fair share right here in New York. But we got us the municipal police set up to deal with it. Works real well most of the time. From the commissioners right down to the patrolmen. Not one man on the force wouldn't like for the carrying of guns by private citizens to be outlawed. But if that ever comes, it won't be for a long time. Best we can do now is enforce the laws we got on the books. And there's a whole bunch of them laws against the kind of shoot out that almost happened here."

"You saying that here in New York a man doesn't have the right to protect himself, Captain?" the half-breed asked.

Gilpatrick finished his drink and ceased to draw against his cigar. He straightened up. "You know what I'm saying, mister," he replied sternly. "You strike me as a man with a brain as sharp as his reflexes so I don't intend to draw you any pictures. The frontier and its ways moved west from here a lot of years ago. And me and every other man in this city who carries a shield are here to make sure those ways don't come back."

Mason Dickens had used his acquaintanceship with the police captain to jump the line and give his statement to a patrolman. Now he returned to stand on the bloodstain which was all that was left to show a man had been killed in the hotel barroom. His pale face continued to express anxiety.

"You through with me?" Edge asked.

Gilpatrick pursed his thick lips around the again dead cigar. "Unless you got any hard information you want to volunteer, mister? That has a bearing on the shooting?"

14

The half-breed said nothing and could not be sure whether or not his silence was an implied lie.

"All right, Mase, get your notebook out." The detective waited until the reporter was ready. The nervous Quinn moved a pace closer. Gilpatrick stared into space as he said, "The municipal police of this district ask members of the public to be on the lookout for the man who shot and killed Vincent G. Powell in the bar of the Fifth Avenue Hotel." He paused to direct his gaze into the impassive face of Edge. "Anyone who thinks he knows or sees the gunman is urged to report the fact to the police and to make no attempt to approach him."

"Is that all, Captain?" Dickens asked as Gilpatrick made to turn around and go to check with the patrolmen.

"What else?" the detective growled. "You were here and you saw what happened. So you've got the killer's description. The victim was a big wheel in the tobacco business so you shouldn't have any trouble digging up some background on him. Hell, Mase, you want me to do your job for you?"

"Captain, couldn't you tell him not to print the name of the hotel?" Quinn put in hurriedly. "He could just call it a mid-town hotel, couldn't he?"

Gilpatrick wore an expression as if he were sucking on a sour lemon. "I could say a whole lot to him, mister. But he's a newspaper scribbler who happened to be at the right place at the right time for a change. So anything I told him wouldn't turn out to be anything like he prints."

Now he did leave the small group at the bar counter and the hotel manager seemed on the point of addressing his plea directly to the reporter. But Dickens spoke first.

"Forget it, Quinn. The *Globe*'s only one paper that'll carry the story. And even if all of them held back on the hotel name, it'd be all over the city by word of mouth. Hell, there wouldn't have been many more people to witness what happened if the killer had rented Madison Square Garden to shoot down Powell."

The manager blinked, gasped and became disconsolate as he realized the truth behind the reporter's exaggeration.

"Shall we get out of here, Edge?" Dickens asked. "I need to file my story with the office. Unless you've got something to tell me that'll give me a head start on what the other sheets will carry tomorrow?"

"Not a thing, feller."

Dickens led the way through the scattering of tables to the doorway.

"Mase going to show you how to get to Grand Central?" Gilpatrick called from where he was seated at a table, leafing through a sheaf of pages torn from the patrolmen's notebooks.

"I know how to get there, feller," the half-breed answered.

"Don't miss your train."

"You telling me?"

"Just trying to cut down on my work, Mr. Edge. We got enough eastern-style trouble here in the city. We can well do without the imported kind. Now beat it, or you'll be late."

"Like Powell's late?"

"Don't think it couldn't happen."

Dickens pulled open one of the double doors and they went out into the crowded lobby. Another patrolman was on duty there, barring entrance to a group of noisy men who immediately began to fire questions at Dickens and Edge. They used the reporter's first name and called the half-breed "cowboy" and were obviously staffmen from competing newspapers.

"No deal, no deal," Dickens repeated as he forced a

way through the press of journalists. "Gilpatrick'll give you a statement."

"He wouldn't give you the pickings of his goddamn nose!" somebody snarled.

"That's because he rolls his stinking cigars out of them," another countered.

They exited through the Broadway doorway of the hotel and both of them relished the fresh, warm night air, pleasant in contrast with the perfumed and smoke-filled atmosphere of the barroom and lobby. The wide street and its flanking sidewalks were crowded with traffic and strollers, impervious to what had happened behind the white marble façade of the large hotel.

"The *Globe* office is over on Seventh at 29th, Edge," Dickens announced. "Faster to walk than to try to get a cab this time of night."

"Lead the way, feller," the half-breed allowed, not interrupting his apparently nonchalant survey of the street and buildings.

The reporter started to walk north on Broadway, looking for a break in the traffic to cross to the other side of the street. "I really appreciate your cooperation, Edge. Hope you don't mind, but I'd like for you to wait for me outside the *Globe* building."

"If you've got carpets down, I won't spit on them."

Dickens shook his head, as preoccupied with private thoughts of the future as was Edge with reflections on the past and staying alert to the present. "It's not that," the reporter muttered. "I'm just a couple of steps up from the kid who makes coffee for the city room. I get all the crumby no-account assignments like the Elks dinner I was supposed to cover tonight. If I let them know in the office the kind of deal I've got with you, they'll take me off the story and give it to somebody else."

17

"Somebody likely to have better contacts than a man who reports Elks dinners, feller?"

"Hell no!" Dickens came back fast. "I've been around this town a long time, Edge. Bad luck is all that's kept me low down on the totem pole."

"A man makes his own luck," the half-breed answered, having to increase his easy walking pace to keep up with the reporter as Dickens ducked out onto the street and began to weave between stalled cabs, carriages, wagons and streetcars.

"What I'm trying to do now, isn't it?"

Edge did not believe anymore in what he had told the tall, thin man striding along at his side. Not in every instance, anyway. Luck—or fate, or destiny, which was how he elected to think of this most variable of indefinable occurrences in life—could often be changed by a man's reactions or responses to a particular event. But just as often it could not be; influences outside his control either ruled the decisions he made, or overruled them.

Luck, fate or destiny had caused Vincent G. Powell to step around Edge tonight and thus stop a bullet which was probably intended to kill the half-breed.

How many other times had the man now called Edge escaped violent death because of the predetermined or involuntary action of the others? The same for the man he once had been—Josiah C. Hedges?

That had been his given and family name during the mostly halcyon days on the Iowa farmstead where he was born and grew up to adulthood. Throughout his youth, violence and the threat of death had made its presence felt on occasions, but raids by marauding Plains Indians had been relatively few and easily beaten off by his parents and then by himself and his younger brother, Jamie. Less frequently, passing strangers had brought danger to the farm. But the closest any member

18

of the Hedges family came to death was when the two boys were playing with what they thought was an empty Starr rifle which exploded a shot when Josiah squeezed the trigger—the bullet shattering Jamie's right leg and making him a cripple for the remainder of his short life.

Their parents died peacefully struck down by disease, and the two sons developed a fine working partnership until the first shots were fired in the War Between the States. Too lame to fight for the Union, Jamie was able to run the farmstead singlehanded while his elder brother rode as a lieutenant, then a captain, in the U.S. Cavalry.

Josiah Hedges was little more than a raw kid when he went to the war, but like so many others who survived, he emerged a hardened and embittered man. Was perhaps affected more than most by his experiences of war. Because under his command had been six troopers who were probably the most vicious and amoral men who ever donned cavalry uniform—men who were often more of a threat to their captain than were the Rebel enemy.

But when the bloody war eventually gave way to an uneasy peace, the mustered-out cavalry captain rode home to Iowa with every intention of forgetting the grim past and making a bright future for himself and Jamie. Until he saw that Jamie had no future—that his kid brother was now just a corpse sprawled in the yard of the burned out farm, the marks of torture on his body in process of being eradicated by the talons and beaks of rapacious buzzards.

Perhaps if the six men who committed the outrage had all ridden away from the farm, the man called Edge would not have been created. But only five had gone, leaving one of their number as dead as Jamie. One ex-trooper who in death revealed the names of the other

19

five who had been inseparable companions throughout the war.

In hunting down the murders of Jamie and avenging his brother's death, the former cavalry captain had used every brutally learned lesson of the war but he no longer wore a uniform to justify his actions. And he killed a man in Kansas who perhaps did not deserve to die. So the law issued wanted posters on him and because of the mispronunciation of his family name by a Mexican, Josiah C. Hedges became Edge. He also became a drifter, at first searching for the opportunity and a place to put down roots, then acknowledging that this was not to be—surrendering to the dictates of his ruling fate which ordained that his destiny lay in survival for its own sake.

Since that day in the June of '65 when he rode up to the burnt out farmstead on the Iowa prairie, this man had never won anything that he was allowed to keep. Women, money, a place to rest his mind and body in comfort and safety, friendship. . . . He had been allowed to enjoy such minor luxuries and reassuring relationships for only cruelly short periods before violence and death intervened to rob him of all that he had except his life. Until eventually he ceased to look for that which other men took for granted.

Violence and death continued to shadow his backtrail or lay ahead in ambush and sometimes he had to endure physical pain. But his decision to forsake the normal human desires at least protected him from the greater agonies of mental anguish and grief. He ate, drank, slept, earned money, had a woman and accepted the help of others whenever or wherever the opportunity presented itself. Coldly. Paying for what he had or returning the favor for favor. So that he could be totally devoid of emotion when what he had was taken from him.

Such a drastic decision to alter the course of his life and the way he lived it owed nothing to luck. But what of all those events which caused him to become hard and embittered enough to make the choice? Jamie's death. The even more harrowing way in which his wife had met her end. The taking of jobs which earned him big money he always lost. The strange circumstances which had brought him to New York. No man could see into the future, so when he was faced with alternatives and committed himself to one or other of the courses open to him, surely he was trusting to luck that he had chosen wisely?

Unless he was a man called Edge who did not give a damn which way the spinning coin came down.

"We'll go down the alley," Mason Dickens said. "Short cut to the *Globe* building. There's a bar in the basement where you can wait for me."

The half-breed nodded his acceptance of the reporter's suggestion and glanced quickly in both directions along the length of West 28th Street before he stepped into the alley behind Dickens. As far as he was able to tell, nobody had followed them from the hotel. But he could not be so sure as he would have been out on the plains or deserts or in the mountain country of the west. In the city there were too many people and too much cover among the buildings. Too much noise and too much cement. And he was prepared to admit that fifty men could be trailing him without him being aware of their intention.

The alley was broad enough to allow a wagon to pass through, enclosed on one side by a towering building and on the other by a high wall broken at intervals by closed gates. The glow from the street gaslights filtered a short way into the darkness at either end. The sounds of the city were muted by the walls. The clack of their footfalls were amplified, by these same confining walls.

The two men who came into the alley behind the half-breed and the reporter wore soft-soled shoes and made fast, secret progress under cover of the distant humming sound which was a composite of all the noises of the great city. So that it was Edge's highly developed sense of the presence of danger rather than any clumsy movement by the men which warned him of their approach.

He did not turn around immediately. Instead continued to move with apparent nonchalance in the wake of Dickens who was six feet ahead of him as he said,

"How long you been a reporter, feller?"

"Ten years." Dickens did not turn around either as he concentrated on avoiding the trash cans and empty cartons and broken packing cases that littered the alley. "Started out on a weekly sheet up in a small Vermont town. Got the job on the *Globe* seven years ago. But I know this city better than most people who've lived here all their lives, Edge."

"Seems you don't know enough to stay out of dark alleys," the half-breed rasped. And came to a sudden halt. Whirled. Drew the Remington. Thought he had timed his move too late.

"Oh, Jesus!" Dickens croaked as he turned to seek the reason for Edge's cryptic comment and saw the attackers.

Big, broadly built men of about thirty dressed in dark shirts and pants which fitted snugly to the muscular flesh of their bodies. Hatless, their faces no more than blobs of paleness in the faint remnants of light which reached this far into the alley. Their teeth gleaming as they grinned in anticipation of an easy triumph. Soures of more intense reflected light were the blades of the knives the men thrust toward the half-breed.

"Beat it, scribbler!" one of the men snarled.

"Just want the cowboy," the other added in a rasping tone.

The first to speak had already fastened a strong grip around Edge's gun hand and forced the Remington to aim uselessly up at the smoke-layered night sky above the city. As he stabbed his knife in an underarm swing toward the belly of his intended victim. While his partner made to lunge around behind Edge to attempt to back stab him.

The half-breed's casual attitude had been a false front while he keyed himself up both mentally and physically to counter the expected attack. So that when he halted and whirled his fear was under control and serving to hone his reflexes even sharper. It was as the fist closed over the wrist of his gun hand and forced the revolver to aim at the sky that his fear expanded at the thought he had delayed his move too long.

Long ago, in the early days of the war which was to teach him so many lessons in the art of survival, such fear in such a situation might well have given way to panic. Now it acted to strengthen his resolve and quicken his responses.

His eyes narrowed to mere glittering slivers which seemed to generate an ice-cold light of their own rather than to reflect that which filtered down the alley from the street. At the same time as his lips thinned and parted to reveal sheened white teeth in the killer's grin.

His legs were apart, his feet firmly to the ground so that he was perfectly balanced. Pitted against two men who were moving, already excited by the prospect of a victory they were sure was theirs.

He threw one leg backwards, swung his body sideways onto the man who trapped his hand, and arched his back. The man snorted with anger as he realized his knife was now aiming at nothing but thin air at the front of Edge's sucked in belly.

"Shit!" the other man snarled as the half-breed's move left him in front of Edge instead of swerving around to be behind him. He pulled up short, half turned and started a stabbing action at the target his partner had missed. But had to jerk back the knife as Edge used his partner's momentum to guide rather than force the man into the intervening space.

"Oh, my sweet Jesus!" Dickens groaned, fear transfixing him to the spot where he had turned at the first sign of danger.

Edge hurled himself backwards, venting a grunt of pain through his clenched teeth as his shoulders hit the building wall. But the man who held him suffered a greater pain—screamed shrilly as he was jerked off balance, knife arm flailing, defenseless against the forceful kick which the half-breed directed at his crotch. He released his grip on the wrist and fought against the impulse to clutch at the source of his agony. Edge brought down his gun hand as his left streaked upward to delve into the long hair at the nape of his neck. And grunted again as the heel of his right hand smashed against the top of a lidless trash can. His fingers involuntarily splayed and the Remington clattered to the cement.

"Get the bastard, Eddy!" the man who had not yet made contact yelled.

Eddy was trying, forcing down the impulse to indulge his pain and drawing back his arm for another knife thrust. Cheered by the fact that the gun was no longer a threat, but puzzled by the half-breed's action in reaching for the back of his neck. Then Eddy gasped his dismay and fear as he saw the reason for the move.

For Edge had drawn an open straight razor from a pouch that was held at the nape of his neck by a beaded thong. Drawn it and was swinging his arm down and out.

Eddy halted his own attack and took a backward

step, raising both arms in self-defense as the blade arched toward him, on a level with his throat. He slammed into the solid bulk of his partner and groaned. Saw the direction of the half-breed's swinging arm change and was too late to parry it. Felt a smarting sensation across his belly and was compelled to look down at himself. His black shirt had been cut open for a length of almost twelve inches, to show the dough white flesh beneath. Then the whiteness was abruptly gone, as the lips of the gash in his belly parted to spew crimson wetness.

"You cut me," he accused, astounded.

"Lost your stomach for this, feller?" Edge rasped, and took deadly advantage of the man's instinctive action of clutching at the ugly wound. By turning his wrist and swinging the razor back in the opposite direction, at a higher level, having to drop into a half crouch so that the blade went beneath the sagging chin to open up a deep cut across the front of Eddy's throat.

The dying man attempted to say something as he fell hard to his knees, dropping his knife. But just a gurgling sound emerged from his lips, followed by a short spurt of blood ejected by the final breath to escape from his windpipe.

Edge stepped to the side and kicked his own gun across the cement before the twitching corpse could pitch against his legs. Eddy's unfeeling head crashed into the trash can.

The dead man's partner stared in horror at the corpse, then raised his eyes to look at the blood dripping blade of the razor.

"Why, you . . ." he started to snarl.

"You fellers did the picking," Edge put in as if replying to a question. Then lunged to the side, reaching out his free hand at full stretch of the arm to wrap it around the butt of the Remington.

25

The man dropped to his haunches and made to topple forward, knife hand above his head for a downward stab. But Mason Dickens had beaten his paralyzing fear by then, ran three strides and lashed out with a booted foot. Whether by intention or accident, his toe crashed into the man's upper arm. To produce a scream of agony and rage and a response from his nervous system which caused his fingers to spring open, flicking the knife several feet away.

Edge was on his back then, in process of folding up and bringing the gun to the aim.

Minus his knife, the man knew he was within a split second of feeling a bullet tunnelling into his flesh, decided that his only slim chance was to lengthen the range. So he powered erect and launched into a run, his injured arm hanging limply at his side.

It looked as if he was going to make good his escape, for in starting his dash for freedom and life he charged aside Dickens, who hit the wall and bounced off, each of these unintended moves rushing him across the half-breed's line of fire.

Edge wasted no more than part of a second with a futile thought about the Winchester rifle that he had left back in his room at the boarding house. Which left plenty of time for him to get into a less awkward posture, thrust the Remington out at full stretch and sight along the top of the barrel.

But the running man did not die from a gunshot. Something which reflected light spun through the air from behind where Edge sat and Dickens squatted on his haunches, the half-breed unmoving and impassive, the reporter gasping for breath. An expertly thrown knife that homed in on the target as if drawn by a magnet—to sink its blade deep into the flesh below the left shoulder bone. The man's run became a stagger, weaving him from side to side. And perhaps he might have made another three yards under the force of forward momentum had not his legs crashed into a pile of cartons, which caused him to pitch full length across the cardboard. As dead and still as his partner.

Edge started to turn his head, but halted the action as he felt a ring of cool metal press into the back of his neck.

"Easy," a man said soothingly. "I'm a friend."

"No, feller," the half-breed answered evenly, looking into the terrified face of Dickens. "Anyone who aims a gun at me is never that. Once I'll allow is a mistake. Twice and I kill him."

The gunman laughed, soft and confident. "Mr. Edge, you just showed you're a hard man. You don't have to prove it with words." He moved the gun muzzle away from the flesh. "That was just to be sure you didn't make a mistake in the heat of the moment. And figure I was with Boss Marlon's men."

Edge had heard the name before. So had Dickens, revealing his knowledge with a short gasp. The reporter stayed down until the half-breed had eased upright and turned to look at the newcomer. A man of about forty, well dressed in a city suit, shirt and tie. He also wore a derby, which he raised in greeting as he spread a warm smile across his weakly handsome face. His gun was out of sight.

"You throw a good knife, feller," Edge said. "But I'm not beholden to you."

A nod as the hat was set on the slicked down hair again. "Appreciate you could have dropped him, Mr. Edge. We use guns here when it's necessary. But they're noisy, are they not? And New York is more crowded with over curious people than the wide open spaces of Texas."

"Tall people come from all over."

"What?"

"I'm from Iowa."

A shrug of the narrow shoulders of the unlikely looking knife thrower. "A figure of speech. Shall we go?"

The half-breed still had the revolver in one hand and the razor in the other. He stooped to wipe the blood off the blade before he returned the razor to the neck pouch, kept his hand draped over the butt of the Remington after he slid the gun into its holster.

"You're not with the police?" Dickens asked nervously, licking his lips and then grimacing as if they tasted bad.

The man broadened his smile. "They'd like me to be, Mr. Dickens. I guess they'd really welcome me for a long stay in the Tombs."

The reporter's anxiety deepened.

"Don't worry about it, Mase," Edge offered. "Nobody can know everybody in a city this big."

The reporter shook his head, then nodded. "If he's not a lawman and after what he just did to a Marlon man, he has to be with Boss Black."

"On the button, scribbler," the knife thrower congratulated. And nodded toward the 29th Street end of the alley as an enclosed carriage turned in off the thoroughfare and moved slowly between the high walls, hauled by two black horses. The finely groomed coats of the animals gleamed as luxuriantly as the brass of their harness and the highly polished coachwork of the post chaise.

"Boss Black is inside?" Dickens asked incredulously, as the horses stepped delicately over the sprawled body of the man with a knife in his back. It was another name Edge knew.

"Sure is. And he'd appreciate you two gentlemen taking a ride with him."

The wheels of the carriage crushed some cartons but missed flesh and bone. There was a liveried driver on the open seat. And another man, not in uniform, standing up in front of the footman's seat at the rear of the enclosed compartment. Both of them were somberfaced.

"We're almost where we want to get to, feller," Edge answered as the driver brought the post chaise to a smooth halt, the horses only three feet from where the men on the ground stood.

The knife thrower became as unsmiling as the men aboard the carriage. "When Boss Black wants something, it doesn't matter at all what other people want."

"I have a murder story to file with the paper," Dickens said, without hope that his excuse would be accepted.

"They playin' hard to get, Sheldon?" a deep voice asked from inside the post chaise. The man moved as he spoke and the vehicle rocked on creaking springs.

"Guess they don't trust us, Black," the knife thrower answered.

"You tell 'em that if they don't do like I want, you'll kill 'em." The deep-voiced man said it as if he were passing a comment on the weather. He sprang open one of the doors. "We can get by without the cowboy and the scribbler we don't even need."

"You better believe what he's saying to you," Sheldon warned.

"I believe it," Dickens muttered and gulped as he shot a sidelong glance at the half-breed.

Edge dropped the hand away from his gun and moved toward the open door. "No sweat, Mase," he growled. "Never have been ready to put my life on the line for other people's beliefs."

Chapter Three

BOSS BLACK was a Negro. Edge saw this as he climbed aboard the unlit post chaise parked in the dark alley. He also saw that the man was grossly fat with a barrel-shaped torso topped by a head that sat on his shoulders with almost no neck intervening.

"You sit alongside me, son," the big black man invited, as Edge entered the carriage.

"What about the dead men?" Dickens asked.

Black snorted. "They worked for Emilio Marlon, didn't they? Means they were garbage. What better place to leave garbage than where they are?"

The blinds were pulled down in front of the windows but as the driver steered the team into a turn, and a change in the mixture and level of sounds from outside further revealed they were out of the alley and on the street, Edge struck a match to light a cigarette he had started to roll as soon as he was aboard. "You ain't tryin' to scare me, are you, son," Black asked evenly, stabbing a short, fat finger toward the Remington on which the half-breed had struck the match.

Edge held the gun in his left hand, resting in his lap, aiming at nothing. Black took hold of his right hand and eased the flaring match toward his own face, to touch the flame to the end of the fresh cigar clenched between his teeth. He held the match there longer than necessary and spoke through his teeth.

"I get it, you get it. The guy ridin' on the back ain't for openin' the door and helpin' me to get outta this rig."

The big man's jet black skin gleamed in the matchlight from the crown of his totally bald head to the lower of several chins which rested on his shirt collar and necktie. The clenched teeth and white surrounds of his eyes provided vivid areas of contrast. Obesity made the head look wider than it was long, the cheeks bulbous, the nostrils flared and the mouth large. The skin was unlined but this did not cause the man to look younger. He was close to sixty. He was attired in evening dress to the extent that he balanced a collapsed opera hat on his thick thighs.

The match flame died and the half-breed pulled his hand out of the big man's grasp to drop the burnt-out stick into an ashtray on the dashboard of the luxuriously appointed vehicle.

"Just didn't want to mark up your nice rig, feller," he answered as he slid the gun back into the holster. "Never have been able to do that trick with the thumbnail. Maybe it's only Texans can do it."

Black laughed and the shaking of his enormous body seemed to be transmitted right down to the springs of the post chaise. "And you're from Iowa, son."

"Anything you don't know about me?"

"Everythin' I need to know." The laughter had ceased and Black's voice was hard and menacing. "For openers, you killed three of my men some place between Denver and here."

The reporter gasped and said, "Oh, my sweet Jesus."

A little street light was now filtering in around the sides of the blinds. The Negro leaned forward to look across the front of Edge at Dickens.

"Didn't he tell you that, scribbler?"

"We didn't have time to talk about anything, Boss Black."

"But he has great expectations," the half-breed put in.

Black grunted and leaned back against the padded seat again. "Listen good, scribbler. Leave it up to you what you put in that lousy sheet you work for. But I guess you're smart enough to know what to leave out. On account that if I read what I don't wanna, you'll get your name in the obituary column. You mind, son?"

"If you kill him?" Edge asked.

Dickens groaned.

"If I tell him why Marlon wants *you* dead?" Black sounded a little impatient.

"Figure I'm more interested in that than Mase is, feller."

"You gotta have some idea, son. After the shoot-out at that railroad depot in the sticks?"

"Marlon got it wrong."

Another laugh, but harsher this time. "He makes a habit of that, son. You seen tonight. Three of his men sent after you and two of 'em dead."

"Hey, I know nothing, remember?" Dickens put in, his eagerness for a good news story serving to diminish his nervousness.

Black blew more aromatic smoke into the eye-stinging atmosphere of the enclosed carriage. "Starts out in Denver, Territory of Colorado. And all happened on account of a crazy old fool named Silas Martin who figured he could steal from me and get away with it . . ."

Black must have known that for Martin it had started in San Francisco, but he chose to skip that part.

For Edge, the beginning of the trip to New York had been up in snow-covered Wyoming where he first saw the three Orientals who he was later to discover worked for a New York crime boss named Black. The trio of

Japanese was dead by then, and Silas Martin had only a few breaths left in his gangrene-poisoned body.

Not until then did the half-breed realize just what he had gotten involved in when he agreed to be Martin's bodyguard on the train trip from Denver to New York State. He had been lied to, but that was nothing new. And he got paid in full and survived, was able to walk away from the bloody slaughter that took place at the railroad depot of a small town in eastern Kansas. When a bunch of Emilio Marlon's men thought they had won the prize of a bejewelled golden buddha—only to be gunned down by an opposing force of Black's men who rode off to New York City with the half-million-dollar statuette.

Edge had headed in the same direction, but with no intention of involving himself further in the conflict between the two New York gang bosses. Simply because he had never been to the city before and thought he might as well take a look at it since he was so close.

Three days amid the bustle and noise and stink of the place had been enough for him and had he not arrived at the Grand Central depot too late to catch the first westbound train of the day, he would already be well advanced on the journey back to the vast open spaces beyond the Mississippi-Missouri which grew more appealing with each moment that elapsed. Out there in the big country he would have been aware that he was being trailed, would have spotted the blond haired kid with the crooked teeth long before the would-be assassin got close enough to try a revolver shot.

But the kid had done him a service. Here in the alien environment of the largest city in the country, the half-breed's highly developed, almost animalistic instincts for sensing danger had not been functioning until the Frontier Colt blasted a misdirected bullet into the Carolina tobacco grower. But that brush with sudden death had jolted Edge out of whatever brand of city-soured carelessness had ailed him, honed him sharp and ready to meet the threat which trailed him into the alley.

"It's as simple as that," Black concluded after giving a well-informed account of what had happened on the violent trip from Colorado to Kansas. "I owned that buddha statue. Had it bought and paid for it in Frisco. First Martin stole it from me. Then Emilio Marlon had his men try to snatch it. I wanted it for my collection. That bastard just figured to make me look like a chump with egg on his face. And to rile me into startin' a war here in New York. But I made him look the chump. Hit him hard out there in the back of beyond."

"And Marlon thinks Edge is to blame for what happened to his men?" Dickens asked.

"On the button, scribbler. When all the time the cowboy was just workin' for old man Martin." Black had been staring at the front panel of the carriage as he told the story. Now he turned his head to rasp directly into the half-breed's ear. "Now I want you to work for me, cowboy."

"Doing what, feller?" Edge crushed out his cigarette in the ashtray.

"A job you oughta enjoy, son. The guy that was shot in the hotel died by mistake. You were meant to get that bullet. On Marlon's orders."

"He already knows that, Black," Dickens said.

The Negro raised a foot and stamped it hard to the floor. In response, the driver called to the horses and steered them to the curb. "Guess he did. And if he didn't, what happened in the alley back there must have made it clear somebody doesn't like havin' him alive and kickin'."

"You want me to kill Marlon, feller?"

The post chaise had come to a halt on what seemed

to be a quiet side street. Hooves rattled on paving and then were silent. Saddle leather creaked as a man dismounted. Footfalls approached the vehicle, the nearside door was pulled open and Sheldon smiled in.

"That ain't for publication, of course, scribbler. Nothin' Emilio Marlon would like better than for it to be known that Boss Black had hired a man to go after him. On account of he's got a lot of big brass law in his pocket. But nobody has to know, do they? Nobody has to know that I've had ten thousand dollars put into the scribbler's bank account which coincidentally he'll pay to somebody called Edge after Marlon's just a hunk of cold meat on a slab in the Bellevue Hospital morgue."

"In my account?" Dickens croaked.

Black showed his big, white teeth in a broad, menacing grin. "You gotta live here in the city, scribbler. And I guess you're smart enough to know it wouldn't be for very long if one penny of that bounty money was spent before it was earned. All right, you can both get off now. I want to be at Booth's Theatre before the curtain goes up." He laughed. "They're doin' Uncle Tom's Cabin. Funniest damn play I ever did see!"

Dickens climbed out of the carriage hurriedly.

"No deal," Edge said evenly.

"Kill him, Sheldon," Black countered in the same level tone of voice.

The weakly handsome man on the sidewalk carried his Frontier Colt in the waistband of his pants. But he had not even started to delve a hand between the plunging lapels of his coat before Edge had slid along the seat to make room, drawn the Remington, cocked it and pressed the muzzle into the folds of fat that were the Negro's series of chins. Black did not quake. Showed fear only in a widening of his eyes.

"I already warned your boy that if he points a gun at

me a second time, I'll kill him," the half-breed rasped. "If he's fast enough, maybe I won't make it. You sure won't."

The exchange had been heard by the liveried driver and the second bodyguard. The post chaise rocked and creaked as both men leapt down to the sidewalk.

"This is stupid!" Black accused, and his fear also sounded in his voice. The many chins wobbled as he forced the words out around his Adam's apple. "What'll it gain either of us if we both get dead, son?"

"I ain't in this for gain, feller," the narrow-eyed half-breed replied. "This gun ain't for hire unless you count me having to use it against people getting in the way of a job I am paid to do. And right now I'm working for nothing. For me."

"Doing what, you crazy sonofabitch?" Sheldon snarled.

"Looking for a blond haired kid who tried to kill me."

"His name's Kirkby, son. Hangs out at a ritzy cat house called the Silver Lady Bar on Park Avenue. But he's a prick. Marlon is the one who pees through him. He's the one you oughta go gunnin' for."

"Do my work my way, feller."

"All right, all right! You've made your point. Appreciate it if you'd take the damn gun out of my neck."

"What then?"

"I'll go to the play and you'll get on with your work."

"Easy as that?"

"Sure." Black was no longer afraid. Looked and sounded as full of confidence as he was before Edge pulled the Remington. "You don't want my money, I'm happy. But I figure I'll still get what I want. If you're as good as a lot that I've heard and the little I've seen."

"Come on, Edge." Dickens urged nervously. "You

36

know what he means. Marlon won't let it rest until either you or he's dead. Especially after what happened in the alley and if you try to kill another of his men."

"Sure he knows that," Black said, easing his head back, away from the gun muzzle, so that he could turn full face and grin at the half-breed. "So we don't have a deal, son. Makes it an even better deal for me."

Edge continued to grip the gun, but without noticeably aiming it at the big man as he slid further along the seat and stepped down from the carriage. Sheldon, the second bodyguard and the driver had their hands under their coats but had not pulled their guns. The post chaise had come to a halt on a deserted residential cross street between two brightly lit avenues. A few lighted, curtained windows broke up the shadowed façades of some of the brownstone houses. It was very quiet, the city's rumble sounding much as it had back in the alley where two men now lay dead.

Black nodded his wish that no one was to die here, for Sheldon and the other two men took the gesture as a signal: Sheldon to mount his black gelding which was hitched to the rear of the carriage, the others to climb up to their respective seats.

"Couple of things, son," Black said as he reached out to hook a hand over the door.

Edge pushed the Remington into the holster and waited in silence.

"Money stays in the scribbler's account until this thing is over, one way or the other. In case you come out on top and figure you deserve gettin' paid for tanglin' with Marlon. Second, I hear that one word gets out about this talk we had, you won't be no problem for Marlon. On account of you'll be dead. When it comes to carryin' a grudge, Emilio Marlon ain't in my league."

The door banged closed, the foot thudded on the

floor and the carriage jerked forward. The two men riding outside ignored Edge and Dickens. Sheldon scowled down from his horse at the half-breed.

"You double cross him and there won't be any place you can hide in, cowboy. All he has to do is put out the word and . . ."

Edge spat a globule of saliva into the street. "I already heard the words, feller. And seen that your boss carries a lot the weight."

Chapter Four

THE Silver Lady Bar was on the east side of Park Avenue, between 54th and 55th Streets, in the basement of a smart-looking five-story apartment block. Mason Dickens had given Edge the precise address with some reluctance since the reporter wanted to go along but first had to get to the *Globe* building to file his account on the killing of Vincent G. Powell at the Fifth Avenue Hotel.

The half-breed was in no mood to waste time. "All right, Mase. I'll find it myself. Then you will have to find me."

Sullenly, Dickens revealed the address. Then added the warning, "Be careful there, Edge. The madam is Fancy Fay and she's the private property of Luigi Orlando, Marlon's godson."

"Ain't the madam that interests me, feller."

Dickens sighed. "What that means is that the place has a lot of protection. And I don't mean it's guarded by a bunch of Seventh Cavalry troopers. Police protection, Edge. Any disturbance at the Silver Lady, it's the customers who get in trouble."

"The whores take precautions, uh?"

Edge had moved away before the reporter could get started on emphasizing his warning, heard from a distance as Dickens yelled his own address which was down on the Lower East Side of Manhattan Island. One of the lighted windows was flung open and a man snarled for the loud-mouth drunk to be quiet.

The half-breed emerged onto Fifth Avenue and hailed a cab to take him to the address on Park.

"That's high price merchandise they sell in there, mister," the cab driver warned as Edge paid him off in front of the pillared porchway of the granite building. "Just thought I'd tell you since you look like you're a stranger in town."

"Obliged, feller."

The elderly driver grimaced at the coins he was given, which totaled the exact fare he had asked for. "Hey, this all?" he called.

Edge halted before he started down the flight of steps under two gaslamps which illuminated the name of the cat house. "What else?"

"Most people give me a little extra." He replaced the grimace with a condescending smile. "A tip."

The half-breed nodded. "Never draw to an inside straight."

He started down the steps.

"Mean bastard!" the cabbie snarled as he flicked the reins to spur the horse into sullen, protesting movement.

"Sure am feeling like one," Edge muttered as he reached the foot of the stone stairway and pushed open two swing doors with circular panes of colored glass in them.

The air beyond the doors smelled richly of expensive perfume and the smoke of high-priced cigars, trapped between wood-paneled walls, a plushly carpeted floor and an ornately carved ceiling. It was a big room, enlarged by knocking down the walls of several smaller ones. A dozen square pillars hung with many oil paintings now kept the apartment building above from collapsing into the basement. All the pictures were nudes, showing smiling, big-breasted women cavorting in idyllic pastoral settings. The bar was a circular arrangement in the center of the room, built around a large piece of stone sculpture which was also a fountain, the sound of splashing water providing a pleasant counterpoint to the soothing music being made by a slim young man seated at a grand piano at the rear of the room. Two other slim young men, similarly dressed in tight-fitting light blue pants and white shirts opened to the waist, tended the bar. There were no tables out in the open, apparently they were in the curtained booths that ran along each side of the room.

"Good evening, sir," one of the bartenders greeted warmly, lisping slightly. "Are you meeting anyone here?"

Like the piano player, the men behind the circular counter were blond haired. But they all had straight teeth and delicate bone structures; and foppish manner- isms which suggested they might scream or even pass out if any of them found it necessary to fire a handgun.

As Edge advanced on the bar he glanced with appar- ent indifference to left and right, noted that outside each draped booth there was a slot with a card fitted into it. Most of the cards were colored green. Low- voiced talk and an occasional laugh or giggle came from some of the booths with a red card in the slot.

"John means do you have an appointment with someone special, sir," the other bartender explained when the half-breed failed to answer. "Or do you wish Madam Fay to call the ladies who are free?"

"Feller who brought me here said they were all high- priced." Edge said as he reached a curve of the bar and eyed the water-run statue. "You've got bourbon?"

"Sure thing," John replied, and crouched to bring a bottle and shot glass from under the counter. He poured the drink.

"How much?"

"Oh, you don't know the arrangements at the Silver Lady, sir?"

"Gentleman's an out-of-towner, John."

"Yes, that's obvious, Philip. The drinks are free, sir. But this is not a drinking establishment, as such. If you wish merely to drink without benefit of pleasant feminine company, you should not be here, sir."

Edge emptied the glass at a single swallow, apparently ignoring the two now anxious-looking faggots as he continued to survey the centerpiece of the fountain. He poured himself another without needing to look at what he was doing as a door opened in back of where the pianist played.

"Was told a feller named Kirkby would be here."

"Rod's out right now," the woman who had entered the room announced as she came around from behind the piano and moved smoothly and sensuously toward Edge. "No telling when he'll be back. But we have some fine ways of filling time here."

"This is Madame Fay," Philip introduced as he placed a stemmed glass and a bottle of wine on the counter top when the woman halted, two feet away from Edge.

"Our clients get to call me Fancy," she offered with a bright, friendly smile that did not quite take all the hardness out of her eyes.

They were brown eyes, matching the color of her elaborately styled hair. Her skin was very pale, a quality she encouraged by the use of a lot of powder. Her mouth was full, like the curves of her body which were emphasized by the contoured stiffness and tightness of the bodice of her flame-red gown, high neck and long-sleeved, wasp-waisted and sweeping full length to the floor. In the low level of light supplied by two gaslit crystal chandeliers she looked to be in her mid-twenties. All woman and proud of it.

42

"I see you're admiring our fountain. It really is quite something, isn't it?"

The sculpture showed two figures. A man and a woman locked in passionate embrace, caressing each other toward blatant arousal.

"It was carved from a solid block of marble by a local New York sculptor. A regular client of the house. We consider him a very fine artist."

"Seems to me he's a dirty chiseler, ma'am," Edge muttered.

Philip had uncorked the bottle and poured red wine into the glass. He and John expressed shock at the half-breed's terse response to the enthusiastic remarks about the sculpture. But the woman almost sprayed a mouthful of wine over the bar counter as she laughed, the sound of her enjoyment and the way she threw her head back an incongruous switch from the decorous attitude she had adopted before. She curtailed the laughter and glanced anxiously along the two lines of draped booths, then grinned and moved closer to Edge, clutching the glass and sliding the bottle along the bartop. The half-breed did a double take at her and even before he smelled her breath he realized she was drunk. The wine was going down on top of rye whisky.

"You're right, stranger. That carving is just plain obscene, isn't it?"

Edge saw an exchange of worried looks between John and Philip. Then snapped his head around as metal rings rattled along a wooden rail. He saw curtains part and a red-headed whore in a low cut dress emerge from one of the booths on the left. She giggled and took a short leap forward as the man rising from the seat behind her slapped her hard on the rear.

"Hey, not in public, honey," the whore chided good-naturedly, and evaded the hands of the short, fat, drunken man as he made a grab for her waist.

43

"Now, now, senator," Fancy Fay rebuked with mock sternness. "Everything comes to he who waits."

"You got no idea how long I have to wait for Kirkby?" Edge asked as the whore took hold of the politician's hand and led him toward the door at the back of the room after closing off the booth and turning the card in the slot to show the green side.

The madam took another sip at the wine, grimaced her distaste for it and set down the glass. "He could walk in through the door any moment or be gone all night. Best you come back tomorrow, unless you want to make use of the services we supply here."

She was a woman of many moods, likely to change at any moment. The taste of the wine after rye had seemed to jolt her into realization that she was drunk. This fact annoyed her and she directed her displeasure toward Edge, having to make an effort to be civil in case he could be persuaded to stay.

"Never have paid for a woman, ma'am."

"Then that means you've never had one! They all get paid for one way or another. Who shall I tell Rod Kirkby is looking for him, mister?"

"He'll know me when he sees me."

The hardness had spread from her eyes to take over her entire face. She looked a lot older now. And dangerous with the smoldering fire of ill temper that was ready to flare into a vicious anger. "Not here, he won't. I'm not in business to supply free liquor for men with time on their hands."

"Why don't you just tell him where he can find Rod, Madam Fay?" John asked.

He and Philip were working to a prearranged plan for dealing with a troublemaker. One had moved to the left around the curve of the bar, the other to the right. When they were fifteen feet apart they came to a stop and rested one hand on the countertop while the other went out of sight below it.

"Like hell I will!" the madam snarled, shrill and loud, her angry tones silencing the sounds of secret pleasure from behind the curtains of the occupied booths. "Get this bummer out of here! He smells of horses and like he hasn't changed his underwear in two months!"

The two free drinks he had swallowed had served to ease some of the tensions out of the half-breed. Tensions which had been seeded by Gilpatrick's questioning and grown rapidly, with no outward signs, between the time the quick-to-smile Sheldon had pressed the Colt muzzle into the back of his neck and when the enforced ride in the darkened carriage ended. Tensions which had nothing to do with being shot at, the knife attack or the deaths of the innocent Powell and two would-be killers. Violence and sudden death left him untouched for they were as much a part of his life as breathing and he had learned to deal with them emotionally as coolly as he handled them physically.

What clenched at his nerves and drew them taut was the time that had been wasted while he meekly conformed to the dictates of city society. First holding still for interrogation by the law, then allowing himself to become a virtual short-term prisoner of the arrogant crime boss. While the man who had shot at him made good his escape into the cement jungle of New York and the man who had ordered the assassination had time to organize and set up another attempt.

This was not the way of the man called Edge. He had almost always handled his own trouble in his own way, preferably without outside help. If a man hit out at him, he hit back. Do unto others as they do unto you. Kill or be killed. One of the few tenets by which he lived not drawn from his wartime experiences. For in war the army chain of command had existed. An order for giving orders which demanded that a man's responsibilities for his own actions should be strictly limited by his rank.

He had understood the need for this, used to advantage the links of the chain of command within the small, tight-knit group of killers he led on missions behind the Rebel lines and even in the hell hole of the Confederate prison camp at Andersonville. For as a captain he was charged with the survival of his men as well as himself. But since the war—or was it only since the terrible death of Beth?—he had had no one to look out for except himself. Apart from the handful of men or women who had paid him to look out for them.

But nobody had bought the protection of his gun here in New York, which was the way he liked it to be, with just his own life on the line and confident that he had what it took to stay alive. But the civilized ways of the city had got to him. In less than three lousy days.

Or was it just this city in that short length of time? Hell, in Denver when he first tied in with Silas Martin after killing the Oriental and an express man who made the mistake of pointing a gun twice in the same direction, peace officers had descended in force to cramp the style of the half-breed. And in other towns all over the west—old towns and new ones that were springing up all the time—a strict code of law and order was being established. A code which insisted on due process of law, practiced by peace officers and judges who were likely to deal as harshly with the second man to draw a gun as the first.

The effect of the two drinks was instantly neutralized by the madam's snarled insult. But the tight ball of rage that began to pulse in the pit of his stomach did not alter any line on his lean face, and his easy stance at the bar with both hands resting easily on the countertop did not change.

"You don't really mean that, ma'am," he said evenly as the extent of his feelings began to show in the intensity of the glitter from his slitted eyes. "Smell of horse or dirty long johns ain't strong enough to rise above the stink of a cow palace."

"Cow palace!" the madam shrieked, as a half dozen pairs of drapes were jerked apart and the shocked or curious faces of the booths' occupants peered through the gaps. "John! Philip! I'm not going to stand here and be . . ."

"So sit!" Edge snarled, bringing both hands away from the countertop.

With his left he reached across the front of his body, splayed the fingers and shoved hard against Fancy Fay's rage contorted face. She screamed in fear and alarm as she was sent staggering backwards, got her feet entangled in the hem of her gown and fell to the carpet.

The pianist banged out a discordant series of notes as he dragged his hands off the keyboard and spun around on the stool.

By that time the half-breed's right hand had fisted around the butt of the Remington and his thumb cocked the hammer as he drew the gun from the holster. On the periphery of his vision he saw that the man at the piano was unarmed and open-mouthed with fear. There was neither the time nor the capability to rake his narrowed eyes over the occupants of the booths. For the two faggot bartenders were hoisting up long-barreled revolvers from under the countertop. And the expressions on the delicately boned faces of the men left no doubt that they were ready, willing and able to use the guns against Edge.

"Don't point them at me!" he rasped as his own gun cleared the holster and he swung it up into view.

"Kill him!" the pained and humiliated madam ordered from the floor as she tried to untangle her smartly booted feet from the torn lining of her dress.

The Remington swung on to John first, as the hammers of both long-bareled guns clicked back. Edge squeezed his trigger and John suddenly had a hole in the center of his exposed chest. A hole that oozed blood as the man was driven backwards by the impact of the bullet—then spurted it as John hit the obscene sculpture, vented a keening wail of pain and fear, and fell forward. The front of his head cracked against the rear side of the countertop and the skin of his brow split open as he collapsed to the floor.

Philip's gun exploded while his partner was still falling, the bullet cutting a furrow across half the countertop and then burrowing through the carpet to imbed itself in the floor beneath. It came within a fraction of an inch of putting a hole through the crown of Edge's Stetson as the half-breed threw himself down to the right.

The faggot had squeezed his eyes tight shut while he fired the shot, perhaps because he hated to use a gun or maybe to blot out the sight of his dying partner. Whichever, when he opened his eyes and failed to see Edge standing at the bar, he felt certain he had scored a hit. And a smile of triumph spread over his features as he leaned forward to look down over the counter.

"You friggin' fool!" Fancy Fay yelled at him, and Philip died with the accusation ringing in his ears.

Edge was lying on his side, the elbow of his right arm hard against the carpet as he prepared to fan the hammer of the Remington with the heel of his left hand—aiming to blast a fusillade of shots through the front of the counter. But he had only to knock back the hammer once and squeeze the trigger as he angled the barrel of the revolver upwards. To send a bullet tunneling into

48

the head of Philip, which had appeared above the top of the counter like a target in a shooting gallery.

The man was hit in the right eye, the bullet passing through his brain to be trapped by the crack it made in the top of the skull. Philip was knocked upright and then backwards, to imitate John's final actions, hitting the statue, coming forward and cracking his forehead on the counter as he went to the floor.

"Oh, my God!"

"Sonofabitch!"

"Murderer!"

"What's happened?"

"He's gotta be crazy!"

The responses to the double killing were yelled by the occupants of the booths and by the whores and their clients who came running into the room through the doorway in back of the piano. Then all sounds in the room save for the splashing of water in the fountain were silenced as Edge got to his feet and swung the gun to aim at Fancy Fay. She had disentangled her legs from the dress and was sitting on the floor with her back pressed to the front of the bar counter.

"Get up, ma'am," the half-breed rasped, as the killer glint in his slitted eyes lost its intensity.

She showed defiance in face of the gun's threat, was apparently not afraid of it. "Make me!"

"You ain't my type," he answered and leaned down.

"No!" a whore gasped, certain Edge intended to put a bullet into the madam at point blank range.

Instead he hooked the long, brown-skinned fingers of his left hand inside the high neckline of her dress and jerked his arm up. The movement was smooth and his impassive face showed no hint of strain as he lifted her like she was no heavier than a loosely packed sack of straw. He raised her high enough so that her feet were

two inches clear of the floor. Then he set her down gently.

"Kill him!" the woman shrieked, emerging from the
terror which had gripped her while he lifted her. More
angry than ever. "Some of you creeps gotta be carrying
guns!"

The whores, their partners and the piano player remained transfixed in their state of shock for a stretched
second more. Until some of the women stared at or
nudged some of the men. Edge snatched a glance
around the plushly furnished room and saw two men
make a move to draw a weapon. He pushed forward his
gun hand to press the muzzle of the revolver hard into
the madam's belly.

His voice was as hard as his eyes as they gazed into
the enraged face of Fancy Fay. "Know the women in
this place are fast. How about you fellers?"

"No!" the madam gasped, tearing her eyes away
from the trap of Edge's gaze to rake them fearfully
around the room.

The half-breed used his left hand against her again.
But this time the fingers were clenched into a fist, the
knuckles of which crashed into the point of her jaw as
she swung her head to look up into his face again. Her
defiant rage had been replaced by fear and then, as the
blow found its mark, her features took on the lines of
repose.

She made no sound as she was driven into unconsciousness. One of the whores vented a short scream
while another snarled an obscenity. Fancy Fay began to
drop limply to the floor, but Edge moved to prevent
this. With the Remington still pressed into her belly,
pinning her to the front of the bar, he bent forward
from the waist and curled his left arm around her back
as her head, arms and torso folded forward. So that,
when he straightened, her feet came up off the floor

and she was draped over his right shoulder. When he turned to start for the doors everyone could see that the gun continued to threaten the madam.

"Ray!" a whore yelled.

"What the hell can I do?" the piano player demanded shrilly, angry and afraid. "John and Phil had guns and look what happened to them!"

Edge had reached the double doors and he turned to look back across the basement room. "Don't plan to hurt her any more unless I have to," he announced flatly.

"So what you takin' her away for?" a man wanted to know.

"You saw it. She fell for me and I swept her off her feet. But she'll be back."

"Whether she is or ain't won't make no difference to what happens to you, cowboy," a whore with dyed blonde hair warned, her mouthline twisted by an ugly sneer. "That's Lu Orlando's woman you got and he . . ."

"Likes me, I figure," the half-breed rasped, kicking open one of the swing doors. "On account of I've taken his Fancy."

Chapter Five

In at least one respect New York City was much like many of the frontier towns Edge had been in. In that people were curious enough to stare at anything out of the ordinary, but reluctant to get involved if it looked as if there was any chance of being hurt.

Thus, many people either walking or riding looked on as the tall, western-dressed man carrying an unstruggling woman over his shoulder emerged from a known brothel and ambled casually along the street to where a line of carriages were parked at the curb. Last in the line was a buggy with the roof raised and he set the woman gently onto the seat before he climbed aboard himself, took up the reins and steered the horse into an unhurried U-turn to drive north up Park Avenue. Nobody saw him holster a revolver after he had settled the woman and perhaps no one realized she was unconscious in the shadow of the buggy's roof, wedged upright between the side of the seat and the powerful frame of the man who drove her. Not until whores and clients spilled up out of the Silver Lady Bar yelling excitedly about murder and abduction did interest heighten in the strange sight recently witnessed. But even then, after the buggy had been lost amid Park Avenue traffic, passers-by hurried on their way, shaking their heads and responding with blank expressions to the questions that were shot at them.

Edge felt as calm inside as he looked, driving the buggy at an easy pace up Park, then along East 63rd, across Madison and Fifth to the fringe of the park. He was in greater danger than ever now, but he knew the reason why the first shot had been fired at him and he had struck back in a situation he had set up himself. Had taken the initiative instead of waiting for Emilio Marlon to make a third attempt on his life.

As he drove into the cool darkness of the park, the half-breed ignored futile contemplation of the possibility that blasting the life out of two men was largely responsible for his peace of mind. If he had not killed them, they would have shot him down. It was as simple as that. The fact that he had experienced elation as he saw the blood spurt and the bodies fall, and would never for part of a second feel remorse about the killings, was something he took for granted. He was the way that he was and had long ago given up trying to force changes upon himself. All that mattered was that the two faggots had drawn first. Whether out in a canyon of the far west or here in the city, the half-breed's response to such a situation would always be the same.

Deep into Central Park, he angled the buggy off the track and halted the horse at the side of a stand of timber a hundred feet back from the shore of an inlet of the lake. The woman groaned as he lifted her down from the seat but was quiet again as he draped her across his shoulder and carried her over to the water. He glanced without apparent interest to left and right, checking that the area was deserted, then tossed Fancy Fay unceremoniously into the shallows of the inlet.

She screamed as the shock of cold water brought her back to awareness. Then flailed at the surface with her arms. Edge dropped down onto his haunches and reached a hand to the back of his neck to draw the razor from its pouch. The woman found her footing in the mud of the lake bottom and rose up, making to wade out of the water. Then she saw the crouched down half-breed and caught the flashes of reflected moonlight off the razor as he stropped it slowly on the palm of a hand. It was as if she had no recollection of what had happened to her until she saw Edge. Then she gasped and stood still, up to her waist in muddy water, and raised a hand to explore the discolored bruise on the side of her jaw.

"You yellow-livered sonofabitch," she hissed. "Did great against a woman, didn't you?"

"You were no problem, ma'am," he answered flatly.

"How many more you have to kill, gettin' me out of the place?"

"Nobody wanted to take a chance on me killing you."

She nodded in arrogant satisfaction. "That's because of who I am, mister. Do you know who I am? I'm engaged to be married to Luigi Orlando. Maybe you don't know who he is, since you come from out in the boondocks and . . ."

"Know who he is," Edge cut in. "Godson of a feller named Marlon who's doing his best to have me killed."

Fancy Fay's confidence increased to the extent that she could show a sneering smile. "You've crossed up Emilio Marlon, mister?"

"He thinks I did."

"Then you're dead, mister. You just ain't fell down yet, that's all."

"Come on out of the lake, ma'am."

"Why the hell should I?"

"You could catch your death. Not from the cold, if I have to get my boots wet."

The defiance drained out of her again, almost as if her fear grew by degrees as she watched the half-breed unfold out of his crouch to his full height, continuing to run the sides of the razor's blade up and down the leather textured skin of his palm.

"You threw me in here," she accused, but her words lacked force. When he made no reply, she brushed strands of her ruined hairdo off her face and asked meekly, "What else do you plan to do to me, mister?"

"Have you carry a message for me, ma'am. You can either listen to what I tell you and remember it. Or I can carve it into your hide."

She shivered and started for the shore. When she stepped onto dry land, she took hold of handfuls of the fabric of her dress and began to squeeze out the muddy water.

"Threats don't mean anythin' to a man like you, do they?" she asked, subdued.

"They bother me. You ready to listen now?"

"I have any choice?"

"You're free, white and over twenty-one."

"Speak your piece." She gave up working on the dress. "This gown cost more than three hundred dollars, you know that?"

"Maybe he'll buy you a new one. If he lives long enough."

"Luigi? What the hell is your beef with Luigi? I thought it was Marlon who wants you out of the way?"

Edge nodded. "That was the way it started out, ma'am. But now it's what's called vice versa. Nothing to do with your kind of vice . . ."

"I know what vice versa means!" Fancy Fay snapped. "If you're givin' me a message, it better be one I can make some sense out of."

Another nod as the woman shivered, solely because of the damp clothing that was clinging against her flesh.

"Figure your feller sees a lot of Marlon?"

"All the time."

"Fine. So you tell Orlando to tell Marlon that he

made a mistake. I was just a feller caught in the middle of the shoot-out between his boys and the ones working for Black."

"Black?" the woman rasped.

"Just listen. You tell Orlando to tell Marlon that the mistake he made was a fatal one after what happened at the hotel and in the alley. I could spend my entire life killing his hired hands. Has to be better for me if I get the top man."

Fancy Fay had been confused while Edge touched on the Kansas shoot-out and mentioned the murder attempts she knew nothing about. Now she threw back her head and laughed. It was a derisive sound.

"You kill Emilio Marlon?" she flung at the half-breed scornfully. "If you're that anxious to commit suicide, why use me for a message carrier, you stupid hick? Shit, it ain't no secret where he lives. He's got one of the biggest estates over on Staten Island." She paused, suddenly worried that this might not be the easy and quick way out she had suspected. "Or did you know that already?"

"Everybody lives and learns, ma'am."

She scowled. "You could have stopped almost anybody on the street and just asked. Instead, you had to kill two men and snatch me. Nothing you can do about John and Philip. What about me?"

"Like for you to lie down on your belly, ma'am."

"What for?" Fear made inroads into her confidence again.

"Keep me from having to hit you again."

"I don't trust you to . . ."

Edge sighed. "Just do like you're told, uh?"

The coldness of his tone and manner persuaded her to comply and she made no sound until he placed a foot on the small of her back and stooped to reach a hand up into the voluminous mass of the sopping wet petticoats. "You perverted sonofa . . ." she began as his hand touched her naked legs, then curtailed the enraged accusation as she felt him yank at the petticoats, then heard the fabric tear. She screwed her head around to glare up at him as he left his foot on her back, put away the razor and began to rip the petticoats into strips. "You're goin' to leave me here?"

"Aim to travel light. No baggage." He stooped again, to force her wrists together at the back, then knotted a length of the torn petticoats around them.

"I'll scream loud enough to bring every patrolman in New . . ." This time her words were cut off by Edge, as he yanked up her head by the damp hair and pulled a length of lacy fabric across her open mouth. She grunted and tried to writhe free, but now he had dropped a knee onto her back and she quickly gave up the struggle as he knotted the gag at the back of her neck. And made no protest by sound or movement when he bound her ankles.

"Obliged to you for the help, ma'am," he told her as he rose.

Her hate-filled eyes directed a stream of tacit obscenities at him. She tried to voice them but succeeded only in venting a babble of unintelligible noises through the lace gag. Then was frightened into a new silence as he picked her up and slumped her over his shoulder again to carry her along the shore to a timber dock where a dozen or so pleasure rowboats were moored. She began to writhe and force words out through the gag once more when he lowered her gently into the bottom of a boat and cast off the line. He touched the brim of his hat as he used a booted foot to shove off the boat, sending it riding smoothly out toward the center of the lake.

"Easy, ma'am," he muttered. "You'll get brought in before your time is up." The gurgling of water along the hull of the boat masked the noises of anger she was making as the half-breed turned and headed back the way he had come. He breathed deeply of the almost fresh air that filled the park, which was the only area of the city where he could relish a sense of freedom. But soon he was back on the paved streets, with the buildings to either side, driving south in the stolen buggy. There were not so many people on the sidewalks and vehicles on the streets now for it was that hour of the night when most people who had gone out had gotten to where they were going. Theatres and restaurants, bars and dance halls, gambling establishments and whorehouses.

But it would be some time yet before that period was reached which Edge liked best. He had been in Washington during the war and San Francisco since then. And places like Omaha and Denver that were cities in the making. But never had he been anywhere that was so crowded with people, so over-developed with buildings and filled with so much raucous noise and so many bad smells as New York. Only in the dead of night, in the hours that preceded the dawn of a new day, did the city become almost silent, the streets virtually deserted and the air reasonably fresh.

"So why the hell ain't you aboard that westbound train, feller?" he chided himself as he gazed sourly along the sheened back of the gray gelding in the buggy shafts and down the narrow length of the building-flanked Whitehall.

But it was merely a rhetorical question that required no answer from a man who knew himself as well as he did. He knew when to back away from trouble when it was not his business, but when somebody tried to kill him—and somebody else had given the order—it was solely his business and to hell with everyone else.

He already knew that the Negro Boss Black had connections in California so it was quite likely that Emilio

58

Marlon could issue orders that would be obeyed far away from New York. But the half-breed was not concerned with other places in the future, except to the extent that when he did leave this cement and stone jungle of the city he did not want to have any reason to remember it.

Somebody had made a mistake—Marlon. Somebody had taken a shot at him and was still alive—Kirkby. A lawman had more or less told him to get out of town—Gilpatrick. Another man, with help, had tried to make the half-breed's business his business—Boss Black. Any of these incidents in isolation might not have been sufficient to hold Edge in this city he hated so much. But in combination he was unable to ignore them. It was like having a rock in his boot, a burr in his pants and a bunch of hornets buzzing around his head all at the same time. He was irritated, in the worst possible way. Which was why he had gunned down two men and beat up on a woman to learn something which Mason Dickens could have told him if he had thought to ask.

He left the stolen buggy on a dark street behind the waterfront and ambled toward the row of ferry houses, eyes searching the signs for one which announced the service to Staten Island. Just as the streets of the city were quiet and sparsely populated at this hour, so was this stretch of the waterfront. But the tall, lean half-breed with the impassive face maintained his alert surveillance on his surroundings while appearing to be totally indifferent to them. Even at the best of times it was in his nature to mistrust every stranger until it was proved beyond doubt that the man or woman posed no threat to him. And this was not the best of times, with four of Marlon's men dead, the woman of his godson possibly still floating aimlessly in the boat on the park lake and Edge still alive and free in the city.

So, after he had paid his ten cents fare, he chose his

seat carefully in the gaslit passenger cabin of the ferry, with his back to a bulkhead and an unobstructed view of all who came, went or stayed. There were not many. A half dozen couples of various ages, two families with three small children each, a group of four young giggling girls and perhaps a score of men in small parties, pairs or alone, all of them looking like home-going workers from office or factory.

Down here at the tip of Manhattan Island, the half-breed's mode of dress drew no curious glances and the only people he saw showing surreptitious interest in him were the four young girls who eyed him from under their bonnets with either coy admiration or grimacing distaste between their bursts of laughter. Every other man in the cabin who was not in his dotage or encumbered with a wife and children received a similar mixture of attention, for the girls had reached that stage of adolescence where their bodies got ideas their minds could not handle.

The man with the cardboard suitcase came aboard just before the ferry cast off from the slip and looked around the uncrowded cabin as if he was searching for somebody in particular. It seemed that he noticed Edge last of all, and smiled brightly as he sank into the seat opposite the half-breed. He was a man just a year or so older than Edge, but in no other way was he similar. He was short, fat around the middle and across the shoulders, pale-skinned and balding. He was dressed in an old and creased suit which was at least a size too small for him and a derby hat which he placed on the seat at his side as he rested the suitcase on his knees. At first glance he merged into the group of ferry passengers as an insignificant nobody. When he was seated, directly under a cone of light from a gas mantel, his dough-colored face set with small black eyes and featured with a bushy red mustache above an almost lipless mouth looked almost diabolically evil. Now the smile seemed not so much bright as brittle.

"Howdy, cowboy. You're a long way from Texas," he greeted in a gravel voice.

Edge pursed his lips. "Once rode with a herd from the Rio Grande to Laramie, feller. But I wasn't punching cows. And a long way from Texas is where I like to be."

The smile stayed in place, showing yellow stained teeth that looked a little big for the mouth where they grew—or were fitted. "My mistake."

"I can forgive and forget."

The ferry was clear of the dock now, changing course across the Upper Bay and being thudded by what was left of the ocean rollers after passing through the Narrows. The man began to lose his composure as the boat juddered, and gripped his suitcase and the seat tightly.

"Not everything, from what I've been hearing, Mr. Edge."

The half-breed showed no physical response to what the man said. "New York's full of surprises."

"Many of them unpleasant in your experience."

"That don't make this city unique, feller."

The man attempted to release the case and push forward a pudgy hand. But the ferry sliced through a big swell and the attempted handshake went by the board. As did the smile, which left his face looking as nondescript as his build and dress. "Name's Lincoln, Mr. Edge. Hell, I hate riding boats."

"Any relation?"

"Too distant to be of any use. I'm just a very small cog in the big Washington machine. You want to play some poker?"

"No."

"Be a good idea if we did. Those three men down at the other end of the cabin."

Edge allowed his narrowed eyes to wander briefly over his fellow passengers and spotted the trio Lincoln meant. All in their mid- to late-twenties, well dressed and recently washed up and shaved. Seated side by side and peering out of the window at the lights of the city with expressions of boredom on their clean-cut faces. The half-breed spent no more time eyeing them than anyone else before he returned his undemonstrative gaze to the sick-looking Lincoln.

"Another unpleasant surprise. Unless you'd spotted them before."

"Seen everyone who came into the cabin, feller. Those three look like they came out of the same mould as some I met in Kansas a while back. Figure they might have Italian names."

Lincoln showed a shadow of his former evil smile. "Don't know their names, but you're right. They're Marlon men. Know all about you."

"Why else would they be aboard this ferry?"

"If we play a little poker it might take their minds off what we're talking about."

"And yours off what's happening to your stomach, feller. No poker. What are we talking about?"

"New York criminals and corrupt New York police, Mr. Edge. And how you can help rid the city of the scum who grow rich in that kind of situation."

"Why?"

"You're not that stupid, Mr. Edge," Lincoln growled impatiently. "These men are in business to make money and . . ."

"Not that way," the half-breed cut in. "Why should I help?"

"Not for money, if that's what you're thinking."

"I'm not thinking anything."

The government man snatched a glance over his

shoulder, along the length of the cabin to where the three well-dressed men sat. One of the trio realized he and his partners had been singled out for special attention and nudged the others, to whisper the news to them.

"Self-interest, Mr. Edge."

"What was that, feller?"

"You were in Kansas at least once before. Just after the end of the war." He stared hard at Edge with his small, crafty looking eyes.

The half-breed's own eyes narrowed to such an extent that it seemed as if he had closed them. And his hands which had been resting easily on the seat to either side of his thighs abruptly clenched into tight fists.

Lincoln smiled his satisfaction that he had at last drawn a response from the tall, lean man seated opposite him. "Thombs," he said softly.

The Civil War veteran Edge—then Josiah C. Hedges—had killed while he hunted the murderers of Jamie. Once before the half-breed had come close to facing up to the legal consequences of that killing. That time, hatred and spite had driven an officer of the law to search him out and attempt to take him back to Kansas.

"Name means something to you, I guess?"

"You ain't guessing, feller."

A nod. "You're right. I've got one of the wanted posters right here in my case. Yellow and curling with age, but it still means what it says. But you can change that, Mr. Edge."

"It never caused me any trouble but the once."

Now a shrug of the broad, flabby shoulders. "But it could. At any time. In Kansas or anywhere else some hungry bounty hunter or eager beaver lawman spots you and recognizes you."

"Like you?"

Edge asked the question of Lincoln, but directed the gaze of his slitted, glinting eyes elsewhere, along the aisle which ran, railroad car fashion, down the center of the cabin. At the three smartly dressed young men who had risen from their seats.

"I was in the bar of the Fifth Avenue Hotel earlier this evening," Lincoln replied, unaware that he had lost most of Edge's attention. "But I was on to you before that. I've had you under surveillance ever since Marlon's and Black's men shot it out in . . ."

The government man broke off as Edge rose lazily to his feet.

"Need to attend to some business, feller."

Lincoln blinked, confused and ready to be angry. But then he thought he knew what the remark meant. "Oh, yeah. It's down at the back somewhere, I think."

But Edge had already gone; abruptly abandoning his pretense of being casual, to swing around, jerk open the door, power outside and slam the door closed behind him. The short, stoutly built Lincoln continued to think he knew the reason for the half-breed's departure—and that the matter had suddenly become urgent. Until one of the three men in the aisle dropped down onto the seat beside him and pressed the muzzle of a revolver into his ribs.

"Don't move, mister," the man rasped out of the side of his mouth, the words faintly accented. "Unless you are in a hurry to meet your maker."

Seasickness threatened to give way to a more violent kind of nausea in Lincoln's tubby belly. But he brought it under control in time to fake a response as he watched the other two men power out of the cabin door. "My goodness," he croaked. "Am I being robbed?"

"You have already lost what we want, mister," the

64

swarthy-complexioned young gunman replied softly. "It had better be that you did not know what you had."

Lincoln remained silent and unmoving as he beat genuine fear and worked to make the man at his side believe he was terrified. As he wondered if he would have a chance to bring out the Frontier Colt which was in the suitcase on his lap. And what it would feel like to fire a gun at a human being again, instead of at targets on the range. He had not done that since he worked for Allan Pinkerton's military intelligence group during the war.

Out on the aft deck of the ferry the two men had come to a tense halt, right hands hidden inside the lapels of their suit jackets as their derby hatted heads swung to left and right, eyes searching for the quarry. The broad-beamed boat had lumbered more than halfway to the end of its journey and was shuddering more violently than ever as it battled against the conflicting currents that raced and whirled at the point where the Narrows met Upper Bay. Far astern the myriad lights of Manhattan threw a glow up into the cloudy sky. Brooklyn to port and the St. George area of Staten Island ahead offered less competition to the moonlight which filtered through the city's cloud cover. Other craft crisscrossed the dark water, some showing just navigation lights, others as emblazoned as the ferry on which death waited to strike.

But the boat carried many pockets of shadowed darkness and it was from one of these that Edge surveyed the men outside the aft door of the cabin. He stood in the cover of a tall ventilation duct that provided air for the engine room immediately below, his right hand draped over the butt of the Remington which jutted from his holster. Immediately to his right was a long lifeboat slung on davits. To his left was an area of open decking that gave access to the second passenger cabin on the other side of the ferry. Beneath and in front of this was the vehicle and livestock section of the boat, with less than half its space taken up by wagons and carriages. Down there, drivers sat hunched on their seats or stood holding the bridles of nervous horses.

No one was on the aft deck except for Edge and two men who intended to kill him.

The thud of the engine and slap of water against the hull might or might not mask the sound of gunfire. The slipways of St. George were still too far distant to offer escape from the ferry if killing shots were heard and a murder hunt was started aboard.

The men moved tentatively forward, easing their guns further from the holsters but not bringing them into view. Their attitudes remained tense as their heads swung from left to right, eyes peering out from under the narrow brims of the derby hats. At the point where the deck broadened to arch out over the vehicle and livestock section, they exchanged hand signals and one continued to move forward while the other quickened his pace to check the port area of the aft deck.

Edge saw this and pulled himself upright against the duct, pressing his back hard to the curving metal. He continued to maintain a light grip on the gun butt with his right hand while his left rasped softly against the six hour growth of dark bristles on his jaw, only inches from where the straight razor nestled in the neck pouch. As was almost always the case, his lean face betrayed no hint of what concerned his mind, which at this time was self anger.

He could overlook the fact that he had failed to be aware that he was under surveillance by Federal agents ever since the carnage at the small railroad town in eastern Kansas. It was the specialized job of such men to merge secretly into the background and if they were all like Lincoln it was understandable why he had been unable to detect their presence. A source of mild irritation, but understandable—particularly since they had posed no threat.

But Marlon's men? They were something else. Totally different from the blond haired kid with crooked teeth and the two knife experts. But, as he had told Lincoln, cut from the same pattern as the bunch which had died in Kansas. He should have spotted them for what they were before he boarded the ferry and forced them into a move against which he could retaliate then. Not waited until the boat was far out into the bay and allowed them to make the first move.

He heard the slow footfalls of the man closest to him and redirected his anger, apportioning it equally between the men who wanted to kill him and the city in which he seemed unable to do anything right.

He eased around the curve of the duct, to a point where he would be in plain sight of the man on the open deck should that man look back over his shoulder. But the smartly dressed Italian with a gun under his coat either had great confidence in his partner or was tensely convinced Edge was on the area of deck that was his province.

The half-breed did a complete circuit of the duct, which placed him behind the closest man who had angled to the side, gun drawn now, to take a look at the tarp-covered interior of the lifeboat, the man's interest drawn by the fact that a section of the cord holding the tarp in place had been cut. He had to climb up onto the deck rail and had one foot on the top and one in mid-air when he either sensed or heard Edge move up behind him. He snapped his head around, then the arm of his gun hand. Which meant he had to release his hold on the davit. He was unbalanced and started to fall back toward the deck. Edge thrust out both arms, hands empty, fingers splayed. His hands curled around the narrow waist of the man, supported his full falling weight, lifted it and then lost it, as the would-be killer swung back up onto the top of the rail, then over it.

"Franco!" he shrieked, and the name lengthened to become a scream of terror as he toppled off the side of the ferry and plunged toward the dark, white-spumed water rushing along the hull.

Edge had gone over the rail in the wake of the falling man, but in a voluntary controlled leap, throwing his legs high and grasping at the top of the rail with both hands. A faint splash below him curtailed the scream. His chest hit the outside of the three bar rail and his legs cracked against the hull. His arms felt as if they were on the point of being wrenched from their sockets. A grunt of pain forced its way between his clenched teeth. Spray from waves that broke against the side of the ferry drenched him with saline water as he lowered himself, hand over hand, until both sets of clawed fingers were hooked over the lower rims of two scuppers. The constant barrage of white water that was flung at him served to warn him, if such a warning was necessary, of the fate that awaited him should he lose his grip. He knew it was too risky to raise himself so that he could see what Franco was doing in response to the calling of his name. And the thudding of the engines and rushing of sea water blanketed all the small sounds.

Franco gave nothing away by shouting out to his partner. He had heard his name but not the diminishing sound of the scream. Had whirled, drawing his gun, and peered tensely at an apparently deserted section of aft deck. Fear raced his heart beats and erupted sweat beads on his face which were immediately dried by the wind blowing in from the ocean. But he was in a dangerous business, experienced enough in it to have learned to control fear, so he did not panic.

He was exposed on open deck, midway between the

port and starboard side. There was a good chance his partner had been taken by the tall Westerner who was causing so much trouble. Less of a chance that the clumsy fool had fallen overboard by accident. He elected to believe the former and chose counter attack rather than retreat. So, eyes darting to left and right in their sockets, the gun thrust out in front of him, Franco moved slowly and silently across the deck, convinced that if the man called Edge was in front of him, he had either to be in the lifeboat or behind the ventilator duct. There was nowhere else for him to hide. If he was there . . .

Franco was as anxious as Edge not to attract the attention of the passengers and crew aboard the ferry, which was why he did not try to flush out his quarry with a shot. He allowed himself a sigh of relief when he reached the cover of the duct, and took time to run the back of his free hand over his sweating brow. Then he sucked in a deep breath and swung fast around the duct, the air rushing out of his lungs when he failed to see the half-breed.

His lips formed into a vicious smile line as he advanced the final few feet to where the lifeboat was slung, rocking gently on the ropes that held it to davits. And the smile broadened when he saw the cords which had been cut by the half-breed's razor. But he was both more cautious and more ingenious than his partner.

He slid the gun back into the holster under his suit jacket and took from a pocket a knife with a blade folded into the handle. He pulled out the blade and began to saw at one of the ropes which held the lifeboat in place, his gaze fixed upon the area of the several fastenings. This placed him just too far back to look directly over the side of the lumbering ferry.

But even had he been closer, he would not have been able to see Edge. For the half-breed, refusing to indulge in the agony of his self-punished arms, had used the scuppers to work his way to the stern. Then, as Franco started to saw at the rope, the chore engaging his entire attention, the half-breed had reached up with first one hand and then the other, and hauled himself, snake-like, under the lower rail to achieve the relative safety of the deck.

Relative because nowhere aboard the ferry would be safe while two of Marlon's men were fellow passengers.

For perhaps ten seconds Edge stayed down, sucking in deep breaths of salty air and resting his aching muscles. Then he rose into a half crouch and stalked toward the Italian, who was muttering softly to himself, anticipating the prospect of seeing the lifeboat crash end-on toward the water—perhaps to snap the other rope and fall upside down into the sea or maybe to simply spill its occupant out through the hole he had himself cut.

The half-breed left his gun in the holster and drew the razor, wrapping his fist around the handle and gripping the blade between thumb and forefinger just in front of the pivot. To guard against snapping the slender, finely honed length of metal as he stepped up behind Franco and sank the blade into the man's back, low down and left of center.

The shock of the wound caused Franco to stretch to his full height as his hands fell away from the rope, the knife slipping from his fingers.

"Too late to launch the lifeboat, feller," Edge said softly as he wrenched the blade out of the flesh. "Your buddy's past saving."

He used his free hand to shove Franco away from him. Paralyzed, the almost dead man was forced to go forward, hit the three bar rails with his legs and folded his head and torso over the top. His feet came up from the deck and, like his partner, he did not start to scream until he was falling through the salt water spray.

Edge kicked the knife over the side in the wake of its owner and then wiped both sides of the razor's blade on the partially severed rope, used it to cut a few more strands before starting to work on the other rope. Then, as he heard the damaged lines begin to creak under the weight of the swaying lifeboat, he started out on an almost complete circuit of the ferry. Across the arch of the stern deck, through the other cabin which was even less crowded than the one he had been in, back over the arch of the forward deck and into the familiar surroundings where Lincoln had approached him.

The government man was still in the same seat, sitting as rigidly upright as the derby-hatted Italian at his side. Both of them had their backs toward the half-breed as Edge moved casually down the aisle. Only the adolescent girls took any notice of him, but pretended not to when he drew close and passed them, perhaps already in possession of the intuition claimed by full-grown women and sensing that this man was one to be aware of.

The seat behind the one on which Lincoln and the Italian sat was vacant and neither of them was aware that it abruptly had an occupant. A man they both had cause to know, who removed his hat as he sat down. If anyone saw this, nobody saw a more surreptitious move, as he slid the Remington from its holster and held it under the hat.

As he made his circuit of the ferry Edge had seen the brightly lit slipway at the St. George dock drawing closer. And as he sat calmly now, aiming the revolver through the back of the seat at the back of a man, he began to wonder if he had misjudged the strength of the damaged ropes which now held the lifeboat in place. For the ferry's engines were suddenly disconnected from the drive, then howled as they were thrown into reverse to slow the boat's momentum.

71

The Italian growled, "Where the hell are they?"

"How should I know, friend?" Lincoln replied.

Because he was listening for the sound, Edge heard the snap of a rope, then another. And recognized both cracks for what they were. But nobody else in the cabin was aware anything was wrong until the much louder noise of the big lifeboat crashing into the sea. And crewmen began to shout.

Anxious looks were exchanged. Questions were asked and not answered. A few people rose and started for the aft door of the cabin. Others were quick to follow.

The Italian was among the first to start to rise. But dropped quickly back to his seat when Edge leaned forward and said into his ear:

"I've got a gun aimed at your backbone, feller."

The mass exodus streamed past within two feet of where the three-man group sat, too intent upon finding out the reason for the worrying sounds from beyond the cabin to be concerned with what was happening inside.

The Italian half turned his head, not surprised to recognize the lean face of the man who threatened him. "This man isn't sitting beside me because he enjoys my company, mister," he countered, unafraid.

The three were left alone in the cabin, the door swinging open and closed with the motion of the ferry. A great many voices were yelling, but not enough and not loud enough. Then a crewman on the bridge decided to sound the siren. Edge raised his gun and removed the Stetson, so as not to put a hole through the hat. He fired the shot into the back of the Italian's neck from a range of no more than two inches. And reached out with his free hand to grip the dead man's throat and keep him from being jerked forward off the seat by the impact of the bullet.

"Yeah, as company he's a dead loss, isn't he, feller?"

the half-breed muttered as he stood up, turned up the collar of the Italian's coat to conceal the blood-oozing wound and tipped the derby forward. So that, to a casual observer, it would look as if the man was slumped low in the seat because he was sleeping peacefully.

"Damn it, Edge," the shocked Lincoln gasped. "You can't just shoot a man dead on a ferry in New York Harbor."

He took a part in the subterfuge by lifting the discarded gun from the seat and pushing it back into the holster under the dead man's suit jacket.

"I just did," the half-breed replied flatly as he turned and started easily down the aisle toward the forward door of the cabin.

Lincoln had to take a few steps at a waddling run to catch up with the taller, leaner man. Outside, they saw that the ferry's master had decided he was too close to the St. George slipway to worry about the lost lifeboat until he had docked his craft.

The government man took several long breaths of the saline smelling night air and this seemed to help calm his jangling nerves. He waited until Edge had rolled and lit a cigarette before he asked, "What happened outside? To the other two men?"

The half-breed glanced out at the choppy water where the Narrows met Upper Bay and spat a loose leaf of tobacco off his thin lower lip. "They went looking for trouble and found it. Now they're in real deep."

Chapter Six

EDGE and Lincoln were the first foot passengers to disembark from the ferry and, long before a roustabout had tried to shake awake the Italian and discovered the man was dead, and the half-breed had rented a horse from a St. George livery stable.

The government man waited outside for him, having given up trying to continue their conversation while he had to half run to match the pace of the striding Edge. Not only the strenuous progress through the streets of the waterfront town disuaded Lincoln; he was also discouraged by the fact that the half-breed's attention was directed elsewhere. Everywhere that one or more men might be lying in wait, eager to succeed at a task which had defeated six others.

When Edge led a big black gelding out of the stable and swung easily up into the saddle, Lincoln rose from where he had been sitting on the end of a water trough. The pale-skinned man with the bushy red mustache had been growing progressively more irritated during the breathless pursuit of the half-breed across town. And this mood had not been soothed as he rested on the stone trough while Edge used up time selecting a horse, taciturn in face of the liveryman's barrage of sales talk.

"You ready to talk turkey now?" Lincoln growled when the half-breed was in the saddle.

"Talking ain't what I do best, feller."

By contrast with Lincoln, Edge seemed totally at ease as he sat astride the big mount on the south side of a small town with a dark night sky overhead and open, rolling country on three sides of him. A man in his element, or as close to his element as he was ever likely to get on the country's eastern seaboard. Despite his ill-temper, Lincoln had the presence of mind and perception to recognize this and his tone remained hard when he said,

"So that old killing in Kansas hasn't bothered you too much, uh? Well, that could turn out to be like a pin-prick to a blast from a double-barrel shotgun if you don't get some kind of official backing for what you're doing here in New York!"

Although the liveryman had doused the kerosene lamp, the door of the stable was still open. He nodded to indicate they should move away from a possible eaves-dropper. And allowed the mounted man to choose the direction, which was down the side of the livery and out beyond the corral in back of it. To a point where the paved street petered out to become a dirt road. The horse made better time than the man on foot, but Edge reined the gelding to a halt and waited patiently for Lincoln.

"I already made a deal tonight."

Lincoln was abruptly interested. "While you were taking the ride with Boss Black?"

Edge pursed his lips. "How many pairs of eyes you got working for you, feller?"

"Not as many as I'd like. But good men."

"Black wanted to pay me for what I planned to do anyway. Sometimes I take that kind of work. When I can't afford to do anything else. So happens my train ticket out of here is bought and paid for."

"So the deal has to be with the newspaper guy. Dickens? What kind of protection can he give you?" Lincoln scowled.

"It ain't that sort of deal. He gives me the cards to play."

Edge guessed the gelding had not been rented out for some time and that probably the only recent exercise he'd had was the run of the corral. For the animal flared his nostrils to suck in night air with its fresh smells of open country. As he scraped at the ground with his forehooves and his flesh quivered, eager to be given a free rein.

Lincoln nodded. "A newspaperman could probably do that. If you took the time to listen to him. But you got a little headstrong after the ride with Black, didn't you? Killed two of Lu Orlando's men and roughed up his woman to get what? An address your tame newspaperman could have given you, for Christ's sake!"

Scorn was mixed in with anger now as Lincoln glared up at the mounted man.

"Washington give a shit about two faggots and a whorehouse keeper, feller?"

The evenly spoken response needled the government man even more. "Washington doesn't condone wanton slaughter, mister!" He moderated his tone to add, "Unless it's necessary."

"Like on the boat? When one of its own was at the wrong end of a Colt?"

Lincoln sighed. "This is getting us nowhere."

Edge stroked the neck of his eager mount. "The horse knows that."

The government man spoke fast to get to his point. "New York City's on the brink of a civil war all of its own. Because two rival gang bosses each wants the city for himself. Black and Marlon. And one of them is going to get it because of certain municipal police chiefs

76

who stand to gain by it. With a quiet life and knowing which boss to go to for their graft."

"It happens all over. Big towns and small ones. Open range, too. Never is room enough for two top . . ."

"Sure, sure!" Lincoln snapped. "You're not the only man around who knows something about human nature. It's bound to happen that either Black or Marlon comes out the winner. But how long is it going to take? And how many innocent people are going to be hurt or killed in the meantime? And what kind of reputation is the city going to have at the end of it? It's not going to be like some range war, mister. With only rocks, trees and the occasional cow being hit by a ricochet. And with only the winner interested in the tract of real estate that's his prize. In the city whenever Black's and Marlon's men shoot it out, people are liable to get caught in the crossfire. And the city's a business and industrial center. As well as being a tourist attraction. But are people going to invest money and tourists going to come and visit in a city that's nothing more than a battleground for power hungry gang bosses?"

Lincoln paused, for breath rather than to allow time for an unnecessary answer. "So the decent and honest men who are involved in running New York want this gang war settled fast and as cleanly as possible. And can't trust their own police force to handle it. So they asked for secret Federal help which is why I and my men came up from Washington."

"Only way to keep a secret is not to tell anyone," Edge murmured, as eager as his horse to be on the move but staying because of Lincoln's earlier mentions of the old Kansas killing.

The government man ignored the remark. "We got here in time to learn something of what was going to happen out at that railroad town in Kansas. And when we saw what happened we got the idea. One big battle, engineered in a way and at a place where we can exercise some control. Let the bastards fight it out. It's too much to hope that they'll wipe each other out. But there's a good chance one bunch will massacre the other."

The half-breed showed a cold grin that had a vaguely mocking quality in the way the lips curled back from the even, white teeth. "You've been reading too many dime western novels, feller."

Lincoln shook his head. "Most interesting thing I've read lately is an old wanted poster."

"With a picture of a feller named Hedges who died a long time ago."

"Amnesty, Edge. With a new flyer going out to every law office in the Union stating the charge against you has been dropped. And to get that you don't have to do very much more than what Boss Black asked. I'd guess."

"Kill Emilio Marlon?"

A nod. "And let his boys think I took up Black's deal?"

"That's just the little more you have to do."

"The decent city fathers like the Negro better than the Italian, uh?"

A shrug. "Just the way the breaks have come. Marlon's gunning for you because he thinks you were on Black's side out in Kansas. And he probably knows Black helped you out in the alley earlier tonight. So it won't be too hard for his men—especially that snotnose godson of his—to believe you're still working for the Negro."

Edge pursed his lips.

"What about it, mister?" Lincoln urged insistently. "It's a powder keg just waiting for the fuse to be lit. But we can't take the risk of Washington being caught with the lighted match. What we can do is bring some indirect pressure to bear on the local law if they try to collar you. So you've got nothing to lose and everything to gain by doing what you plan to do anyway. But doing it Uncle Sam's way. Which is to make sure Luigi Orlando believes you're working for the Negro."

"The godson and godfather are pretty close, uh?"

"Related, even. Orlando's the Boss's nephew."

"Just like me and my Uncle Sam," Edge murmured sardonically, lifting the reins from around the saddlehorn.

Lincoln showed a humorless smile. "Makes it a sort of family affair."

The half-breed clucked to the eager horse and heeled him into an immediate canter. He growled to himself, "With all the outsiders thinking I'm a Black hand."

Chapter Seven

WHILE they had been waiting for the ferry to dock at the slipway, Edge had asked Lincoln where exactly on the island Emilio Marlon lived and the government man had supplied the information freely. In a colonial-style mansion on the southeast shore of the island set in an estate surrounded on three sides by a ten-foot-high stone wall with Lower New York Bay beyond grassy sand dunes guarding it on the unwalled side.

By following the directions the government man had given him, the half-breed traveled for the most part along open trails flanked by pastureland. Just occasionally riding through small towns that looked peaceful and prosperous. Places where the more fortunate men forced to work in the city could return at night and on weekends to rest and breathe air permeated with the pleasant scents of the ocean and countryside. The kind of places—similar in some respects to certain Western towns Edge had passed through—where a man who was unshaven, dressed in workaday clothing and with the knowledge of blood on his hands could feel at ill-at-ease. If that man had once had ambition to live a quiet life in a freshly painted frame house with lace curtains hung at the clean windows standing in a neatly kept garden enclosed by a picket fence in a good state of repair.

But on a night like this one, when his mind was filled with the prospect of killing an enemy, Edge had neither the time nor the inclination to consider with bitter regret what might have been. For all that mattered was what was to be.

It was after midnight when he reached the point where two lengths of high wall met at a right angle. And fifteen minutes later at the horse's walking pace when he reached the double wrought-iron gates set into the wall. He saw the woman sitting on the grassy knoll to one side of the gateway long before he had ridden close enough to attract her attention. There was something eagerly hopeful in her attitude as she watched his approach. But the way he sat the gelding and his impassive face under the brim of his hat lessened the fire of her enthusiasm when he halted the horse a few feet from her and she got to her feet.

She was about twenty, with a pretty face framed by long, jet-black hair. Short and full-bodied, the generosity of her curves shown by the tight fit of the bodice of the white dress she wore. A dress that had been ripped at the center of the neckline so that instead of displaying just the top halves of her breast, it also revealed the full depth and length of the valley between them. She made no attempt at false modesty by holding the fabric of the dress together.

"This the place where Emilio Marlon hangs out too, ma'am," the half-breed asked, touching the brim of his hat.

"You got the right place, mister," the woman answered sourly. "Turned out to be the wrong one for me. Tonight. Guess you ain't in the mood to sell me that horse?"

Edge eyed her reflectively from head to toe. "Dressed like that, I guess you carry money in your garters."

She shook her head. "I don't have no money. That's

81

why you have to be in the mood. All I got to pay you with is me. Name's Belle."

"Get called Liberty Belle, I figure."

"I ain't anybody's!" she flung back at him.

"But you got to have a crack," he answered, swinging down from the gelding and leading the horse by the bridle over to where the iron gates met at the center under a curved stone arch.

"Ain't locked, mister," Belle offered, calming her irritation with him and attempting to repair any damage she may have done. "But you better have been invited. Nobody goes in there unless they're invited. There oughta be a sign on the gates. Saying: KEEP OUT, SURVIVORS WILL BE PROSECUTED. The people in there ain't friendly."

The half-breed tested the simple latch and discovered it lifted easily. "You got a torn dress, ma'am," he said. "But your hide looks in good shape."

The woman sagged down onto the knoll again, placed her bent elbows on her splayed thighs and rested her chin in her cupped hands. "I'm lucky, I guess. Work at one of Lu Orlando's houses. Lu brought me out here into the sticks to a party. Party! Gees! Him and his uncle got into an argument and that creep Marlon started to take it out on me. Wasn't for Lu, I don't know what. Got thrown outta the house. But nobody told the dumb guards that look out for people not supposed to be the other side of the wall. Twice I almost got shot. I been waitin' here more than an hour for Lu to show."

She had started out replying to Edge's comment but then had begun talking to try to release some of her pent-up bad feelings for Marlon and Orlando. It was obvious she was not the smartest whore in New York and was too involved with her own position to consider that she was revealing information that might get her killed. It was almost as if she had forgotten somebody was listening to her, for she looked up with a start when Edge tapped her on the bare shoulder. Then she flashed a bright smile and rose quickly to her feet when he held the reins of the gelding toward her.

"Need a favor, ma'am. Not one of the kind you trade in."

Her happiness waned faster than it had waxed. "You ain't supposed to be here, are you, mister? If it wasn't that way, you'd just ride up to the house and to hell with the guards."

The half-breed pointed a brown-skinned finger toward a stand of sycamores fifty feet back from the gateway on the other side of the dirt road. "You take him over there and wait with him until I come out. Then I'll return the favor. Let you ride with me back to the ferry town."

She was no longer merely dejected. Nervous anxiety showed in every line of her face. "What if Lu comes out first?"

"Didn't bother you when you were ready to trade a ride for a ride."

She searched for another route of escape. "What if you don't come out?"

"Give it to sun-up, ma'am. Then take the horse back to town. He belongs at the Carter Livery. Feller there wanted me to leave money. More than the rental. Told him my word was better than money. Hate to have to break it."

"What'll it matter if you don't come out, mister?" Belle said morosely. "That'll mean you're dead."

Edge showed her a bleak grin that curled back his lips from his teeth but failed to add warmth to the glittering slits of his eyes. "I been told I've got haunting looks, ma'am," he said as he turned and moved toward the gates.

He waited there, watching as the whore started to walk miserably out across the road in the direction of the timber, after tugging angrily on the reins to stir the gelding into movement. Then he went under the arch and closed the gates softly behind him.

A gravel road curved this way and that through unspoiled terrain of rises and hollows liberally featured with trees and brush which grew naturally. For perhaps a quarter mile. Then the twenty-foot-wide gravel ran straight as an arrow between perfectly flat, close-cropped areas of seeded lawn broken by flowerbeds, ponds and clumps of exotic shrubs, finished at a large circle of gravel fronting the two-story, two-winged house which was about a half mile from the gateway. Two windows of the house showed light, both of them to the right of the pillared porch. The soft glow which filtered out through the curtains fell across a carriage with a pair of horses in the traces which was parked on the turning area. Wood-smoke rose from a chimney, pale against the dark clouds, adding a faint familiar scent to the damp, salty air which the ocean breeze wafted across the big estate.

The lawns looked like dark-colored expanses of velvet in the dim moonlight, smooth and unsullied by the booted feet of men. Certainly nobody moved across them now, the guards the whore had spoken of either in the cover of the house or the trees. To the south and north the tree line advanced closer to the mansion than at the west facing front and the half-breed elected to go to his right, his hand hanging close to but not touching the butt of the holstered Remington. He placed his feet lightly in the long, lush meadow grass, eyes constantly moving in their slitted sockets and ears strained to pick up sounds made by men who had no reason to be as cautious as he.

He was in back of the house, heading for the end of a stable block, when he heard soft-spoken voices and altered his course to move toward their source. He did not halt until he was in the deep shadow of a leafy oak tree from where he could see one man and listen to the talk of two. One standing outside a door in the stable wall, midway along the block. The second on the other side of the door. The bad smell which the salt breeze just failed to mask made it evident that there was a latrine on the other side of the door.

"Breasts like friggin' melons, Rico. Wouldn't you say that's what she had?"

"Yes, I would say that, Mario."

"And he kicks her out."

"Yes, he kicked her out."

The man outside was the one who was enthusiastic as he talked about Belle. A short, olive-skinned man with a wiry build dressed in dark pants, dark shirt and dark vest. Tieless, the collar of the shirt unfastened. With a revolver in a holster under his left armpit. And a repeater rifle canted to his right shoulder.

The man in the latrine agreed with him in the dull tones of somebody with something else on his mind.

"But Mr. Marlon." The man outside leaned against the wall and sighed. "What is one more woman to him?"

"Yes, what is one more woman?" the man inside agreed. And broke wind. Then emptied his bowels with a sound like the first torrent of a flash storm.

Mario grinned, as if sharing Rico's pleasure in gaining relief. Then voiced a low curse and grimaced when he caught the stench. He moved along the rear of the stable block, rested his rifle against the wall and took out a tailor-made cigarette and a match. When he turned to strike the match on the stone wall, Edge powered into four long strides which took him into a clump of shrubs at the angle of the rear and side walls of the stable.

The two Italians were talking again, their voices louder now that Mario had retreated from the stronger smell coming out of the latrine. Making crude jokes about the reason for Rico's diarrhea. Then the man outside began to get irritably impatient and their exchanges grew heated, spoken in their native tongue.

Under cover of the bickering, the half-breed used the vines of a strongly growing climbing plant to reach the shallow-pitched roof of the stable block and inched along on hands and knees until he was immediately above where Mario stood, the aromatic smoke from his cigarette marking the Italian's position.

He eased the Remington from his holster and waited until Mario had finished talking and Rico was launched into a defensive response. Then he leaned forward, over the eaves of the stable block roof, and swung the revolver, hand fisted around the barrel so that the base of the butt crashed against the crown of Mario's head. The man groaned softly and corkscrewed to the ground.

Edge landed on the soft grass a moment later, while Rico was still talking. And worked fast, jerking off the pants of the unconscious man and using them to tie up Mario, one leg around his ankles and the other lashing the wrists. He used the razor to cut off a sleeve of the man's shirt and this formed a tightly fastened gag.

Rico had become anxious by now, the tone of the foreign words he spoke revealing that he was calling questions, asking Mario why he had gone quiet.

Edge took Mario's Colt from the shoulder holster and hurled it twenty yards into a thickly planted flowerbed. Then holstered his own hand-gun, picked up the Winchester and advanced on the door of the latrine. Reached it just as it was flung open and Rico emerged, still fastening the front of his pants while he vented vehement Italian curses. He came to a sudden halt, curtailed what he was saying and raised his head to show a terrified expression as the muzzle of the rifle prodded his belly.

He was in the same early thirties age group as Mario. But taller and more thickset. And wore a suit jacket, bulging under the left armpit. His rifle was held loose in the crook of his arm, slid out easily when Edge tugged at the barrel. The stench from behind him seemed to have a palpable presence in the darkness of the latrine.

"Mario?" Rico croaked.

"He'll live, feller," the half-breed replied, backing off and moving his head to indicate the Italian should advance at the same pace. "You want to share in his luck?"

Rico stepped outside the latrine and looked toward where the trussed-up Mario lay. Edge threw the spare rifle through the open doorway. It landed with a dull splash, as if in soft mud.

"What do you want?" Rico had recovered from the initial shock and no longer seemed so frightened. He had pulled back his shoulders and spread a hard expression across his dark-skinned, finely cut features.

"Answers to questions. Like how many more like you are in and around the house?"

"I will tell you nothing!" Rasping and defiant.

Edge sighed, drew back the rifle a few inches, then thrust it forward. The muzzle thudded into Rico's belly and the Italian groaned his pain and bent from the waist, clutching with both hands at the source of his agony. The half-breed side-stepped, raised the rifle and brought the barrel down across the nape of the man's neck.

Rico was not unconscious. But stunned enough so that he had no control over his muscles. Edge had time

87

to dispose of the second rifle in the same manner as the first, then catch the Italian before he pitched to the ground, drag him around and haul him by the slack at the back of his jacket into the darkness of the latrine. Smell guided the half-breed to the lip of the trench which ran along the rear of the place where he stooped beside Rico and made a more secure prisoner of him by pressing a knee hard into the small of the man's back. Rico coughed and gagged toward a recovery as his head was forced over the side of the trench so that his face was only an inch or so above the slime of human excrement.

Edge had to fight his own urge toward nausea as his nostrils filled with the evil stench. "Same question, feller."

Rico tried to struggle but he was already weakened by the two blows from the rifle and the foul atmosphere threatened to put him completely out.

"Just Mario and me in the garden," he croaked. "Two more guards in the house."

"Other people?"

"Mr. Marlon and Mr. Orlando."

"I know about them. Servants?"

"Just women. Cook and three maids. Get me out of here! I'm going to be . . ."

He showered vomit into the trench, to add a new equally foul smell to the thick atmosphere. And continued to retch, marking his trail with the contents of his stomach as Edge dragged him back into the fresh, open air. He lay exhausted and fighting for breath while the half-breed took the revolver from the shoulder holster and tossed it into the latrine before closing the door. He abandoned his attempt at ineffectual struggle and had to be content with muttering soft and venomous Italian curses as he was tied up in the same way as Mario.

Edge had to cut away the jacket sleeve to reach the shirt.

Rico became as silent as the half-breed but expressed total misery in contrast to Edge's confident determination as the razor was replaced in the pouch. Then he groaned, "You might just as well kill me. Mario, too. Mr. Marlon will have us executed for this failure."

Edge lowered the gag toward the vomit-run mouth of the Italian. "Aim to kill Marlon, feller," he said. "What this is all about."

Rico squeezed his eyes closed, as if to prevent tears from spilling. "Then Orlando. Orlando is worse."

Edge laid the gag across the mouth to force the whispering voice into silence, then jerked up the man's head and knotted the silken fabric tightly at the back of the neck. "Seems I dropped you in the shit anyway," he muttered.

Rico snapped open his eyes and for a moment they expressed horror at a vivid memory which crowded into his mind. Then hopelessness filled the eyes.

Edge looked from Rico to Mario and back, both men trussed up with their own trousers. "Just not your night, is it? You and your partner both. You're bound to be caught with your pants down."

Chapter Eight

CERTAIN that the unfortunate Rico had told him the truth about the number of people inside and outside of the house, Edge altered his plan of approach to the place. He abandoned his intention of entering secretly through the rear and instead moved in on the front. Stealthily at first, setting his booted feet down lightly on the gravel as he crossed the area where the carriage was parked, the two-horse team standing quietly in the traces. He ignored the big, nail-studded oak door at the top of the broad flight of entrance steps and moved through the shrubbery to first one lighted window and then the next.

Both were in the same room, hung with lacy curtains that allowed him a blurred view of the furnishings, decor and the two men who were surrounded by luxury. A high-ceilinged room with many paintings hung on the encrusted papered walls. The floor was covered with deep pile carpet. The many pieces of furniture were of dark-stained, highly polished hardwood, the easy chairs deeply padded.

The men sat in two such chairs, one either side of a large fireplace with a grate which was piled with unlit logs. The brandy balloons they held glinted with the many facets of crystal in the light from a chandelier which hung from the center of the moulded ceiling. They were not talking as Edge peered into the room, but the expressions on their faces gave a clear indication of the pattern their earlier conversation had taken. The older man had been bawling out the younger and now the former was trying to calm his temper while the latter continued to smart from the tongue-lashing.

Emilio Marlon was about sixty years old, short and thick-set with silver-gray hair that served to emphasize the Latin coloration of his wrinkled skin. His face was handsome and distinguished, the features square-cut and suggesting great strength of character. He was freshly shaven and groomed, attired in formal evening dress.

His nephew was similarly well turned out. Tall and slender and thus vastly different in build from his uncle. He was also handsome, but although Orlando was in his mid-thirties there was a certain immaturity in the composition of his features. His skin was smooth and despite the olive tones of his heritage somehow had a pasty look to it, as if he seldom exposed himself to sunlight. Only vaguely in the angles of his profile did he bear a family resemblance to his uncle. His hair was jet black, slicked down with pomade and had thinned to give him a high forehead.

He sipped at his brandy as though it were a bad-tasting medicine. Then choked on it as glass shattered and lengths of timber snapped. The shockingly loud sounds made by the half-breed as he hurled himself sideways-on through one of the high many-paned windows. Edge's left shoulder took the brunt of the impact as he sprung up from a half crouch, chin tucked down on his chest, hat at an angle to protect his face from flying glass. Then his thighs and knees were jarred as he folded his legs to enlarge the hole. He kept his hands deep in the pockets of his coat until he was in mid-air and dropping to the carpet through the billowing lace curtain and the shower of glass shards. Then, as he hit

91

the floor on his side, he jerked his right knee free, drew the Remington and rolled over once before coming up into a crouch, gun aimed at Emilio Marlon.

"Don't they have doors in those wide-open western spaces, Edge?" the crime boss asked, sounding as if his composure had not been shaken by a part of degree by the half-breed's violent entrance.

Edge straightened to his full height, gun steady but narrowed eyes flicking between the two men at either side of the fireplace and the closed double doors that obviously gave access to the room from the hallway. Footfalls were thudding toward the other side of the doors.

There was no interruption of the cadence as the running men hit the doors, bursting them open and slamming them back against the wall to either side. Like Edge, they used their left shoulders to force entrance into the room, but they had their guns already drawn.

Marlon made no move nor uttered any sound to issue an order. Would probably not have had time to convey even a hint of his wishes to the men, anyway. For, as the shirt-sleeved, food-chewing man saw the intruder and skidded to a halt on the threshold of the room, their gun hands swung and their trigger fingers became taut and white.

The instinct to protect Boss Marlon was too strong to allow time for thought. And so they did not even spare a glance toward the fireplace to check for that hint. A man was in the room and had no right to be there. A man they doubtless recognized as an enemy of Emilio Marlon. A man who had somehow got past them and their partners to force a way in.

Edge shot one through the heart a split second before both men fired their Colts. And dropped down onto his haunches to explode a shot at the second. This took the man in the right shoulder and spun him. The injured man had time to cock his Colt and start to bring it back to the aim before a third bullet from the Remington drilled through his neck. He gargled on his blood as he staggered to the side, bounced off the jamb and collapsed across the body of his partner in the doorway. Both Colts continued to be gripped by the dead hands of the corpses. The bullets they had exploded were lodged at angles into the plaster at the side of the smashed window.

"There are doors everywhere, feller," the half-breed muttered, straightening up again and resuming his aim at Marlon. "Trouble is, you can never tell what's on the other side of them. You can see what I mean?"

The advent of sudden death into his luxurious surroundings had pierced Marlon's veneer of calmness. But, whereas Orlando was more frightened than ever, the older man was gripped by an intense rage. He tried to raise the balloon glass to his lips to take some brandy, but his grip tightened suddenly and the crystal broke, dropping shards, liquor and blood from his hand into his lap. The man looked down at this, then at his hand. And in a few seconds of time this took, he brought himself under control.

"And to think that I have just been berating my godson for trying to have you killed," he said softly.

Of all the obviously Italian men the half-breed had come across since becoming involved with the New York crime boss, Emilio Marlon revealed least about his heritage with the spoken word. His voice was virtually free of any accent.

"Uncle, I told you . . ."

"Shut you, mouth, Luigi!" Marlon cut in on his nervous nephew, his tone biting.

"You're not just trying to talk your way back from the grave, are you, feller?" Edge posed, conscious that to anyone outside he would be a fine target in silhouette

93

against the light. So he moved away from the window to put his back to the wall. In a position where he could watch both men at the fireplace and also had a clear view of the doorway with two corpses sprawled atop each other on the threshold. There was no reason not to continue to trust what Rico had told him. But it could be that the female servants in the house were as frantically loyal to Marlon as the bodyguards had been.

The net curtains billowed slightly in stray breezes which curved around the sides and front of the house from the ocean. No sounds advanced into the room from the lighted hallway beyond where the bodies lay.

Marlon shook his head. "Not with lies. I do not lie. Perhaps would only consider doing so in order to protect my godson, who I love very dearly." He sucked at the several small cuts in the palm of his hand while he carefully picked splinters of glass from his lap and tossed them delicately onto the unlit logs in the grate.

"Uncle!" Orlando gasped. He had thrown the brandy down his throat in one and it had failed to steady his nerves. He looked paler than ever and on the verge of a paroxysm of trembling.

"Hold your tongue, my boy," Marlon ordered with less vehemence than before. Then looked questioningly at Edge. "In a situation where life is cheap there has to be some other currency of value."

"You're gonna buy him off!" Orlando blurted, relief flooding across his soft, strangely younger-than-its-years face.

Marlon sighed, then with one glance from eyes that were briefly cold and hard drove his nephew back into fear. "With a man such as this," he said, looking at and talking about the half-breed, "it cannot be money. For this man cannot be bought. So I suggest truth."

The older man's dark eyes requested a sign of agreement from Edge, who kept the Remington at its new target of Luigi Orlando but provided a response of sorts by not squeezing the trigger.

"The boy thinks as highly of me as I of him," Marlon went on. "He was seeking only to please me by arranging for you to be killed."

The 'boy' of at least thirty-five years gasped.

"Thoughtful of him," the half-breed growled sardonically.

Marlon nodded, but his expression made it a negative gesture. "In one sense of the word, yes. But in another, Luigi did not think at all. He is inclined to be impetuous. There are many who continue to have this fault far beyond the years of youth."

He looked pointedly toward the billowing curtains and the broken glass and splintered pieces of window frame below.

"It ain't me you have to make excuses for, feller," Edge said.

"Quite true," Marlon agreed. "Luigi, bring me another brandy. I'll need a fresh glass."

Orlando looked fearfully toward the tall, lean, slit-eyed man who was aiming a cocked revolver at him.

"Do as I tell you, boy," Marlon insisted. "He will not harm you. Nor me. If he wishes to live to see another day."

"That a boast or a truth, feller?" Edge asked.

"If we do not deal in truth, this conversation is pointless." He nodded to his godson, who rose cautiously from the thickly upholstered chair and moved across the room to where some decanters and glasses were set out on a wheeled trolley. Orlando did not shift his anxious gaze away from the half-breed until he had to concentrate on pouring brandy from a decanter into a balloon. Edge tracked his moves with the gun. "You have killed four of my men tonight," Marlon continued.

"Five," Edge corrected.

Confusion threatened the older man's composure. "These two. Mario and . . ."

"These two plus three aboard the ferry. The two outside are lying down. They won't need laying out."

"On the ferry?" Marlon snapped, and held off accepting the fresh drink from Orlando as if he feared his new rage might cause him to break another glass. Then he controlled himself and nodded for his godson to resume his seat. He took a sip of the brandy. "Those men were not looking for you to kill you. They had a message to give you."

"I never got it."

"Because you never gave them a chance?"

"Just didn't want to be on the receiving end of anything fellers like that might have in mind to give me."

Another sigh, to signal that Marlon had calmed himself. "In view of what happened earlier, I can understand your attitude. I should have thought of that aspect and kept Franco and the others here at the house. Spoken to you personally as I am now." He shook his head, his face showing an expression of regret, whether for the deaths of his men or his own error of judgment, it was impossible to say. "Those three. Peasants. No finesse." He glanced at the two dead men on the threshold of the room and then at Orlando, including them in the point he was making. "It would perhaps have been better for all of them if they had remained in Sicily to grow grapes for the wine."

Edge briefly recalled the deadly cat and mouse game aboard the lumbering ferry and experienced no sense of regret over the triple killing. Boss Marlon's men had looked nothing at all like message bringers. If a mistake had been made, they had made it.

"We've got the dead head count right, feller," the half-breed said. "You want to pick up where you left off about why this feller shouldn't be numbered among them?"

Orlando clutched tightly at the padded arms of the chair and stared hopelessly toward the liquor-laden trolley.

"Yes, of course. Truth rather than opinions. You were partially responsible for the slaughter of the men I sent to obtain a valuable *objet d'art* which is now in the possession of that nigger Black."

He paused, expecting an interruption from Edge. Perhaps a denial. But the half-breed did Lincoln a favor of saying nothing.

"When I heard of what had happened and of your involvement I was not happy. Not happy at all. And when I am not happy, everyone who is close to me knows of it. Unfortunately, not everyone who is close to me has learned that I prefer to deal with my own troubles in my own way."

He directed a damning glare toward his godson, who pressed himself further back into the deep armchair. And Orlando remained in his cringing attitude for several seconds after the older man had directed his attention back toward Edge.

"And that nigger and the men who do his dirty work are a great trouble to me. Which I intend to deal with in my own time and in my own way. And my way of dealing with trouble is to attack the root of it. Not lop off unimportant branches, one at a time. In the bars of hotels and back alleys."

Orlando was in receipt of another withering glare and reacted in the same way as before.

"No offense intended," Marlon assured Edge. "But in terms of what is happening in New York, a single fast gun from Texas is a snap of the fingers."

He snapped his fingers.

"Iowa, feller," Edge said.

"What?"

"I've been to Texas, is all. I was born and bred in Iowa."

"No matter."

"It does to me."

"All right!" Marlon snarled impatiently. "I apologize for the mistake."

Edge nodded toward Orlando. "It's his mistake we're talking about."

"Not so much a mistake as an error of judgment, I think. Much as the one you made in killing my men on the ferry from Manhattan. Luigi knew I was very angry about what happened and when he heard that the man called Edge was in New York he thought he would be doing me a favor by arranging for your execution. Now, since we are speaking the truth, I will admit that if he had succeeded, I would undoubtedly have been pleased with him. But all he has achieved is to get two of his own and five of my men killed. Which will stir up public anger about slaughter on the streets and cause the city police to . . ."

"Your problem," the half-breed put in. "Mine ain't so big. But a lot more important. To me."

"You will not solve it by putting a bullet in my godson, Edge!" Marlon said with heavy menace. "Which I do not think you want to do in any case. What I think you want is the taste of revenge and then to get back out to Texas or Iowa or wherever."

"I got simple tastes," Edge allowed.

"Then they have been satisfied, I would say!" Marlon came back quickly, with a glint of triumph in his dark eyes. "The lives of seven men in payment for two failed attempts on your own. It is not a bargain I am entirely happy with, but if you are prepared to accept it,

98

I will put my seal on it. Give you my word of honor that if there are any other threats to your life before you leave New York, they will not be as a result of orders issued by me—or anyone close to me."

Orlando had just gotten over the shock of hearing his godfather talk about Edge putting a bullet into him. Now he swallowed hard again and fresh sweat beaded his forehead as the cold, hard eyes of Marlon stared at him. The expression on the older man's face did not alter at all when he swung his attention back to the half-breed.

"What is the alternative? For you to kill Luigi to sweeten your revenge. Then to kill me because you know I would then become a threat to you. Two valid reasons for a man like you to kill. But you are not sure how valid they are in this instance, are you? Or else you would have gunned us down as you came through the window. Or even have shot us from outside. You needed this talk to make up your mind. And if it is not yet made up, I will repeat what I told you earlier. If you wish to live and see another sunrise, then you will leave this house without further violence. Because if you don't you'll become a target for every man who works for my organization. And that's a whole lot of men, cowboy!"

As Marlon warmed to his subject, so his cultured accent suffered; he contracted words and his voice held undertones of his Italian extraction. He abruptly became aware of this and while he paused it was almost possible to see his face as he struggled to calm his feelings.

"But nobody is perfect," he went on, now sounding well-bred and well-read again. "My judgment of you is based upon what I have heard about you and this brief time I have seen you. So it could be unsound. Perhaps you did not come here for personal reasons. Maybe you are still in the pay of the nigger. In which event you run the risk of Black having you killed for making this deal with me."

He smiled and the expression gave him the look of some well-fed animal of prey content to pass up the chance of an easy capture. A patronizing smile.

"Uncle, don't argue against your own case," Orlando urged nervously.

This interruption by his godson did not anger the older man. "If the whole truth is not told, then a lie is implied, my boy," he explained. "So I tell Edge everything so that he is in full possession of all the facts before he makes up his mind. More facts, more truths. If he killed us, who will know? My nigger servants. Mario and Rico. Will he kill these, too? Or leave the servants to free Mario and Rico who will spread the news of our deaths? So he kills all of these? That whore you brought here so foolishly in the belief that she would help appease my anger? Is she dead, or will she have to be killed? I am a businessman with many interests. I receive reports from these interests. People will come and our bodies will be found. It is well-known that this man called Edge thinks he has reason to kill me."

A shrug of the broad shoulders. "Perhaps I exaggerated the truth. Perhaps he will live to see one more sunrise. But most certainly just one. He will be dead before that sun sets." He had been looking at the half-breed but responding to Orlando's comment. Now he spoke pointedly to Edge: "Your decision?"

Emilio Marlon's judgment had been good and soundly based upon the fact that Edge had not crashed into the room shooting. For ever since the blond haired youngster with crooked teeth had blasted the wrong man in the bar of the Fifth Avenue Hotel, there had been a doubt in the mind of the half-breed about who was ultimately responsible for the murder attempt that went wrong. The man who hired only smartly-dressed, smoothly groomed Italians with guns in shoulder holsters and methods designed to attract the least attention from outsiders. Or an eager-beaver, anxious-to-impress kid-after-his-time who used a trigger-happy bad shot and two brawn-without-brains knifemen.

Now he was sure, for there was no option but to believe Marlon. But if he believed that part, he also had to believe the threat which the older man had so calmly spoken.

"A contract which has no need to be written and signed," Marlon urged. "Provided the words exchanged are true. For instance, that you have not damaged my . . . interests more than I know of and you have admitted."

Edge nodded at Orlando. "Shot a couple of people at one of his places. Cat house called the Silver Lady Bar on Park . . ."

"Fay!" Orlando blurted, pushing down with his hands on the arms of the chair. "Have you hurt my . . ."

He powered erect and launched into an enraged charge across the room, fists clenched at the ends of swinging arms, face contorted by a mixture of anxiety and anger.

"Don't be crazy, boy!" Marlon snarled, and had to fight against the pain of age-stiffened limbs to get to his feet. Then he realized there was nothing he could do or say to halt the reckless move of his godson. And his eyes became filled with pathetic pleading as they swung to fix upon the impassive face of Edge.

The Remington was still aimed at Orlando, until the moment the almost hysterical man was close enough to swing two wild punches. Then it was pulled up and to the side, became a short club as the barrel was laid across the nape of Orlando's neck. Edge having slid fast along the wall and folded away from it just as his attacker came to an unbalanced halt and turned to try to redirect the blows. The gun hit the man hard enough to stun him and to crash his head against the wall, this second impact driving his brain into unconsciousness. He fell into an untidy heap at the angle of the wall and the floor.

Emilio Marlon sank back into the depths of his chair with a long sigh of relief and squeezed his eyes tight shut for stretched seconds. When he opened them they showed a hard expression.

"If you killed that slut of his who runs the bordello, I can't guarantee Luigi will keep his part of the bargain."

"Bruised her a little is all."

"So who did you shoot that you neglected to mention before, cowboy?"

"We were talking about men that time."

Marlon looked surprised. "Two of Fancy Fay's whores?"

"Couple of men's men, feller."

The man sucked a final drop of brandy from his balloon, then shook his head. "That boy certainly does get mixed up with some strange people. But he's my dead sister's son. The only blood relation I have left I have to look out for him." He had been staring down into his empty glass. Now he looked up suddenly and seemed to be embarrassed, as if he realized he had spoken aloud thoughts he would rather have kept private. "We have a deal, Edge?"

The half-breed had been holding the Remington loosely at his side since he cracked it against the head of Orlando. Now he slid it into the holster. "If we didn't, your only relation would be spilling some of that family blood now, feller."

"So get out of here, cowboy! And if you have the guts to report back to that nigger Black, you tell him I hold him responsible for all the trouble you've caused. And that he'll pay for it. Sooner rather than later."

Again Edge played it the way the government man wanted it to the extent of not enlightening Marlon about his relationship—or lack of it—with the Negro. Instead, he held aside a billowing curtain and stepped over the sill and out of the room into the ocean-smelling darkness beyond.

"Matilda!" Emilio Marlon yelled. "Get in here and be quick! Luigi's been hurt!"

"But he'll live," the half-breed told Mario and Rico as the two men aimed their retrieved rifles across the gravel area at the front of the house.

They had taken their time to put their pants back on, but even across a distance of several yards and with the breeze blowing freshly off the nearby ocean, Edge could smell that the Italians had not cleaned off the Winchesters after taking them from the trench in the latrine. But it was hatred for the man in the rifle sights rather than the stench of the weapons which moulded the features of their faces into matching expressions of brutal evil.

The taller and more thickset Rico had to speak soft, calming words to still his partner's finger on the trigger. Then called: *"Capo!* We can finish him now!"

Edge did not turn around as he heard footfalls in the room behind him. The fast, light tread of women running. And the slow, heavy steps of an arthritic man. A little more light fell out of the broken window across the half-breed as the net curtain was jerked aside.

"Your apologies for bodyguards allowed him to enter my house!" Marlon said, his voice taut with controlled anger. "And I was forced to give him my word I would allow him to leave!"

Their expressions suddenly chastened, Mario and Rico allowed the rifles to sag, the stocks still against their shoulders but the muzzles aimed at the ground.

"Either of you fellers ever point a gun at me again, squeeze the trigger," Edge said tautly. "An unfriendly warning."

"Not like that, woman!" Marlon snarled as he released the curtain and turned painfully to take over the tending of his godson's bruised head. "I'll do it. Clean up the broken glass! You fools out there! Come inside and get rid of the corpses!"

With their boss otherwise engaged, the two hapless men on the lawn had started to glower their hatred toward the half-breed again, perhaps not even hearing what he said to them as their emotions expanded, made more powerful by frustration and the knowledge that others of their kind were newly dead.

"One of the advantages of being self-employed," Edge said as the tension eased out of him. Tension aroused when the slime-covered rifles were aimed at him and his life had depended entirely upon whether or not Emilio Marlon was a man of his word. "Man can make his own decisions about who to kill."

Mario rasped a soft-spoken insult in his native tongue.

Rico injected a tone of embittered scorn into his voice to counter Edge's cynical claim. "You did not kill those you came here to . . ."

"Get in here, I said!" Marlon snarled.

"But best leave the rifles outside," the half-breed advised sourly as the two men moved to obey the command. "Figure I already raised enough of a stink in there."

Chapter Nine

THE black-haired whore was waiting where Edge had told her but did not emerge from the stand of sycamores until he had dropped and stepped on the cigarette he was smoking and called out her name. Then she approached him nervously, leading the rented gelding, still not bothering to hold together the two sides of her torn bodice.

"What happened?" she asked in an awed whisper. "I heard some shots, didn't I?"

The half-breed swung up into the saddle and then freed a stirrup and offered an arm for her to cling to so she could climb up and sit astride behind him.

"It was them or me, ma'am," he told her, heeling the horse into an easy walk along the dirt road.

"Mr. Marlon and Lu?" she gasped. And held him more tightly around the waist, pressing her near naked breasts and the side of her face hard against his back. She sounded both afraid and excited.

"No."

"Didn't nothin' happen to you?"

"Nothing to speak of."

"Won't they come after you?"

"If they do, you're between me and them."

She caught her breath and snapped her head around to look back toward the gateway in the high wall. Then she laughed. "But they won't. Mr. Marlon give you his word, didn't he? Way you ain't in no hurry is proof of that. And when Mr. Marlon gives you his word, he don't never break it. He's famous for that. A real mean bastard in everythin' else, but he don't never go back on a promise."

"I already got that message."

"Well, I was just tellin' you . . ."

"Ma'am."

"Yeah?"

"I'm a man who keeps his word, too. Sometimes I like to keep all of them. To myself."

"You don't wanna talk, uh?"

"Like I said, nothing happened to speak of."

"Pardon me for livin'," she growled sullenly.

"No sweat. If you can get to like the quiet life."

After that, there was just the steady clop of the gelding's hooves to disturb the peace of the dark night which would probably have been warm had it not been for the chill air pushing gently in off the ocean. Briefly, Edge reflected on his actions and reactions at the Marlon mansion and reached the conclusion that he had done the right thing. Not for Boss Black who was owed nothing anyway. Not for Mason Dickens, but what had the lanky newspaperman done to deserve a favor? And not for Lincoln, who had made a promise he would not now have to keep. But for himself. He had backed off for the very good reason that he wanted to go on living. And he believed what Emilio Marlon had warned about the consequences of more shooting at the house. And immunity from the lethal wrath of every Italian in New York who carried a short-barrel Colt in a shoulder holster was a better deal than amnesty on an ancient murder charge.

Edge curtailed this line of thinking, tried to push it out of his mind but knew this was not possible. The memories of the events which took place and the words which had been exchanged at the Marlon mansion would remain in the dark recesses at the back of his mind. To emerge into the forefront of his consciousness at the most unexpected of times, a constant reminder that he had accepted a compromise to save his own skin, and then had sought to do something which was an impossible as blotting it out of his mind. He had tried to rationalize it.

Glinting lights pinpricked the darkness ahead to mark out the position of St. George and the whore relaxed the tightness of her encircling grip around the half-breed's waist.

"You're city and hate the country, uh?" he asked.

Without needing to look back at her, he knew the sound of his voice after a long silence had surprised the woman.

"Yeah. Oh, yeah. Damn right, mister. Opposite for you, I guess. You comin' from . . ."

"Iowa," he put in.

"I was gonna say the wide-open spaces."

"Figured you might say from Texas."

"Hell, no. You don't talk the way them Texans do. Bunch of them come into the Silver Lady a while back. Cowpunchers."

"You being a whore, is everything from Texas bigger and better?"

She snorted. "Men are men, mister. Somethin' about my John wasn't big, though. And that was his friggin' heart. Had his thirty minutes of fun and when I ask for the twenty bucks it was like I'd asked for a hundred and twenty. Said that anywhere in Texas he could screw a whore to hell and back for a quarter than much."

"Could be," Edge replied as he steered the gelding along the alley and out onto the street in front of the darkened livery stable. "Hell ain't too far from anywhere in Texas."

He reined in and swung a leg over the neck of the horse to dismount. Then, as he reached up to help down the woman, he received an unobstructed view of the complete half orbs of her breasts, the torn dress gaping with the forward cant of her body. She smiled her gratitude and then the expression became professionally sensual.

"It's ten cents for the ferry fare, mister. So I ain't about to charge Silver Lady prices."

He delved a hand into a pants pocket to bring out some coins as he gripped the bridle of the gelding. He gave her two nickels. "For holding my horse back there, ma'am."

His tone was as icy as the glint in his narrowed eyes, his manner far removed from what it had been while they talked over the last few yards of the ride from the Marlon house.

"Man, you sure blow hot and cold, don't you?" she snarled as he raised the latch on the livery door. "Way I see it, a man who kills guys ain't got no reason to lord it over a woman who sells herself to them!"

"You're right."

"So what the hell?"

"So ships in the night, ma'am," Edge called softly from inside the livery as he unsaddled the gelding.

"Who the hell are you?" Belle asked, abruptly switching her irritation with the man inside the livery toward somebody out on the street.

"Friend of Mr. Edge."

The half-breed dropped his hand away from the butt of the holstered Remington as he recognized the voice of Lincoln.

"He's got friends?" the woman said sarcastically.

"He do that to you?" Lincoln posed, pointing to the torn dress as Edge emerged from the stable and closed the door behind him.

"No, mister," she retorted, and glared meanly at the half-breed before she whirled and flounced across the street. "All he wanted me for was to hold his damn horse," she trailed after her.

"How did you make out at the Marlon place?" the government man asked anxiously, moving away from the store front where he had been waiting for Edge to return.

"Guess you could say I held my own, feller," the half-breed replied, and grinned bleakly in the wake of the scorned whore.

"You do what I asked?" Lincoln demanded, grim-faced, and hurried to catch up with Edge who had started out across the street.

"Didn't tell them I wasn't on Black's payroll."

"Tell who?"

"Marlon and Orlando."

"You didn't kill either one of them?"

"Couple of Marlon's boys is all."

"And the *Capo* let you ride away from there with one of his godson's whores?" Lincoln was not quite sure if he was getting straight answers or if the tall, lean Westerner was working up to another joke.

"He kicked out Belle before I got to the house, feller. We made a deal. Orlando's life for mine."

"Deal? How? Why?" The government man was getting angry, the emotion acting to add to his breathlessness as he had to half run to keep pace with the lazily walking half-breed.

"Marlon doesn't want the kind of wholesale shoot-out you're trying to engineer. He was willing to blame Orlando for me killing his men. If I'd call it quits and not kill anymore. Especially not kill Orlando."

"What about our deal?" Lincoln demanded. "The amnesty I offered to . . ."

"Did I agree, feller?"

"Not in so many words, but . . ."

They had reached the ferry slip as the Manhattan-bound boat sirened the intention to leave. Edge spurted away from Lincoln to buy a ticket from the booth and reach the gangway before it could be hauled in. So that the government man had to give chase again, after yelling at the ticket seller to hand over the cardboard suitcase left in his care. The short, flabby man was panting worse than ever as he leapt aboard and waddled over to where the half-breed stood at a deck rail, rolling a cigarette.

"You're a double-dealing sonofabitch, mister!" he snarled through clenched teeth.

Edge waited until he had rolled and lit the cigarette before he turned his head to look away from the slickly dark surface of the water and down into the scowling face of Lincoln. At first glance his own features seemed set in an expression of repose. But on closer inspection the mouthline with the cigarette angled from one end was formed into a vicious thinness and the threaded glints in the almost closed eyes were piercingly menacing through the rising tobacco smoke.

"You going to arrest me for that Kansas killing, feller?"

Lincoln flinched, as if each word rasped through the near lipless mouth was something palpable and pointed, stabbing into the flesh of his face. "Of course not," he blurted.

"Uncle Sam got a whole bunch of city dude gunslingers around this town looking to collect the reward on me?"

"You know not." Then his mood brightened. "Hey, you had to say yes to the deal to save your skin. But now you're in the clear we can approach it from a different angle."

"Word for word, feller."

"What you had in mind?" Lincoln could even grin now, as Edge released him from the trap of the hooded eyes to peer out over the water again.

"No," came the response with a shake of the head. "Marlon gave me his word. I gave him mine."

"Then may you hang in Kansas!" the government man snarled, spun on his heels and stormed into the cabin.

"However it happens, there has to be a better place to go than here," the half-breed growled, looking balefully toward the approaching lights in the closely packed buildings at the lower tip of Manhattan Island.

He remained out on deck for the whole trip, aware of somebody standing in the shadows of a stack of life rafts. Knowing who it was and sensing the animosity that was being directed toward him. Impotent animosity. But, as the ferry altered course and reduced speed to nose into the slip, the twenty-dollar whore approached the half-breed with a brittle smile across her face.

"Hi there, again. I got the same problem I had on the other side."

Edge glanced at her and saw that she had managed to get some pins from somewhere and that she was now more or less decently covered.

"Me, too," he said absently, her words breaking in on his train of troubled thought.

"But I need more than ten cents now. For cab fare up to the Silver Lady."

The ferry bumped to a stop and the vehicle ramp was dropped as gangways were slid aboard.

"Suggest you take out the pins, ma'am," Edge muttered as he moved away. "They say it pays to advertise."

She rasped an obscenity in his wake but he had already closed his mind to the whore. And to everybody else and everything that was not a potential danger to him as he disembarked from the uncrowded ferry and gave a cab driver the address of Mason Dickens' apartment.

"Thank God for that," the bearded, weary-eyed man said, his voice thick with a Scots accent.

"Yeah, I know," Edge answered, dropping a cigarette stub into a pool of horsewet in the gutter. "You were worried I might want you to take me back to Texas."

"Guess there are other places out west," the driver allowed as the half-breed climbed aboard and peered out of the open window, scanning the ferry slips exit for the familiar short, tubby form of Lincoln.

Then the reins were slapped above the back of the horse in the shafts and the cab was steered into a tight turn to head north. It was going home time for the people who had been out on the town and as the places of entertainment spilled their occupants, the sidewalks and streets filled up. And the noises and smells of too many people living too close together wafted in through the window.

Hearing the sounds, smelling the odors and watching the press of people and crush of traffic, Edge murmured, "Texas doesn't seem like so bad a place anymore."

And abruptly found himself wondering why he made a habit of running down the state and the people who lived there. He had had some bad times in Texas and some run-ins with a few mean Texans. But no more so than in other states and territories, and he had had to fight for his life against people from all over. No, his anti-Texas jibes were just a contribution to the American joke, a lighthearted defense against the boastful claims of those who were natives of the biggest state in the Union.

New York? Edge could see how it might be fashionable for out-of-towners to hate the city. But in his case, his attitude was based upon a much deeper foundation than what happened to be the vogue. Nor, like is cynicism toward Texas, did it have anything to do with being shot at and having to fight off attackers with knives. He hated New York because here in the city he felt stifled, both mentally and physically. He sensed he was a foreigner in his own country and for some strange reason this inhibited him—to the extent that he felt he could not be himself. Was afraid to be himself?

That was the key word. Afraid. And in the private darkness of the cab the half-breed scowled his disgust as his mind finally released this self-admission which he had tried to bury beneath a brittle weight of rationalization. Luigi Orlando was still alive because the man called Edge had been too scared to keep him. Afraid of the power of Emilio Marlon. A man who might also be dead now, if the confrontation had been out in some frontier town, in the rugged mountains or on a limitless prairie or desert. Where Edge would not have stopped to consider how many loyal gun hands Marlon had working for him, would have given no thought to the kind of terrain he had to cover to escape the consequences of reaping his revenge.

"Here you are, cowboy," the cabbie called as he reined in the horse. "Delancy and Lewis. Dollar."

Edge climbed down from the cab and reached up to drop two coins into the driver's outstretched hand.

"You tried, but I ain't a stranger in this town anymore, feller," the half-breed growled as the bearded driver scowled at the dime and nickel in the palm of his gloved hand.

Then the man shrugged and pocketed the money. "Flat fare. Nothin' extra?"

"You aimed to cheat me. What's that worth?" His tone and expression were neutral.

The driver set his horse into motion with an angry gesture and Edge allowed himself a brief smile of satisfaction as he made to enter the apartment building where Mason Dickens lived. Then abruptly altered course and instead strolled along the empty sidewalk. Walked the deserted streets for perhaps two hours, until he was sure that the nagging doubt which had been needling him since he left the Marlon mansion—causing the sullen mood which was vented through his churlish displays of ill-temper with the defenseless whore and the innocent government man—was eradicated. He had admitted, could understand and therefore accepted the reason for the course of action he took out on Staten Island. And because of the state of mind with which this left him, an avaricious but otherwise harmless cab driver had been allowed to leave without witnessing the killer glint in the slitted eyes of Edge.

Mason Dickens lived on the third floor of the brownstone building, reached by flights of dimly gaslit wooden stairs which creaked at every tread. The plastered walls were cracked and stained with damp patches. The air, which felt colder here than out on the street, smelled of food cooked hours ago, cat-wet and disillusion. No sounds came from behind any of the doors on each bare landing. And only at the base of the door to the newspaperman's apartment was there a strip of brighter light than that which was emitted by the gas mantles.

Edge rapped his knuckles on the door panel.

"Who is it?" Dickens sounded nervous.

"Nobody from Texas."

Dickens' footfalls approached fast and the door was jerked open. The man's pale face beneath the unruly mop of light-colored hair blatantly showed the depth of the anxiety which had sounded in his voice. He had changed out of his evening suit into a pair of baggy,

114

stained pants and a collarless shirt with the sleeves rolled up to his elbows. His black encircled eyes were too bright and there was a strong smell of rye on his breath.

"How come you're still running around loose?" he demanded, and thrust his head outside to peer down the stairway before stepping back and beckoning for Edge to enter the apartment.

"Who wants me?" the half-breed asked, glancing around the room as Dickens closed and locked the door.

It was a living room with one corner serving as the kitchen and just a single door leading off it, obviously to a bedroom. Spartanly furnished with ancient pieces of furniture. Badly decorated, untidy and uncleaned in a long time. The temporary home of a man who lived without a woman and spent most of his time away from the place.

"Captain Gilpatrick, that's who!" Dickens rasped as Edge dropped into a deep armchair with several splits and flat areas in its leather covering. "For killing the two barkeeps at the Silver Lady and leaving Fancy Fay bobbing around in that boat on the lake in Central Park. You're crazy, Edge! I warned you, damnit! I told you that place has police protection! Hell, Gilpatrick spends more time in that whorehouse than in his office at headquarters!"

Edge took off his hat and rubbed the back of a hand over the stubble on his jaw as he yawned. "The killings were self-defense. Needed some information from the madam."

Dickens was pacing up and down the room. Then he stopped and sat wearily on a swivel-chair in front of a paper-littered roll-top desk against a wall. He turned the chair so that he could look across to where the half-breed sat. The tension of pent-up anxiety drained out of

115

him, as if he were suddenly too exhausted to play host to powerful emotions.

"Where did the information get you?" he asked flatly.

Edge shook his head. "None of your business, feller. It never has been anybody's but mine and Marlon's ever since the kid took a shot at me at the hotel."

The reporter made to interrupt, but the half-breed shook his head again. "Just listen. New York's a big town and big towns have lots of people in them. A lot of people make a lot of noise. With their mouths mostly. Tends to confuse a country bumpkin like me."

"Bumpkin!" Dickens snorted.

"Mase?"

"Yeah?"

"I just got out of a bad mood. I'm feeling good. Don't change it, feller."

"What d'you expect from me, mister?" Dickens growled. "I'm hoping for the story of a journalistic lifetime from you. Not a cowboy's reflections on the big city!"

"Don't want a thing from you," Edge replied, eventoned in contrast to the other man's irritation. "Just figured I owe you an explanation. You don't want it, I'll leave."

Dickens sighed, then picked up an unsharpened pencil which he began to roll between the fingers of both hands.

"First Gilpatrick butted in on my business. Then you. Next Black. A feller from Washington."

The newspaperman was suddenly interested. But Edge continued without amplifying his oblique reference to Lincoln. "All of them trying to get something for themselves by interfering in my business. So by the time I got to the man I had to do business with, I was one confused country boy in the big city."

"You got to Emilio Marlon?" Incredulity spread across Dickens' face with the speed of a lightning flash.

"Sure."

"What happened?"

"I finally got to realize that New York people are the same as people any place else, feller. They want to stay alive and they want to live easy. I scared the hell out of Marlon and he got to me in the same way. And after that we finished our business by making the only kind of deal worth making. Because we both had something the other one wanted. Marlon to keep his godson alive and me to go on living. Rest of you people just wanted to use me for your own ends. Because none of you had the guts to go and get the shit scared out of you by facing up to Marlon."

He put his hat back on and pushed himself up from the chair.

"Just like that, uh?" Dickens said.

"What like what, feller?"

"You kill a few men, give Boss Black the idea you've got a deal with him and then walk out on him, rough up a whorehouse madam with a police captain in her pocket . . . all that and you reckon you can just go up to Grand Central and wait for a train west."

Edge nodded and went to the door.

"Maybe in Tombstone or Dodge City or some other hick town out west, mister!" Dickens snarled, worry displaced by anger as he realized he was about to lose the chance of the big story he had planned to get. "But never in a million years here in New York City. It doesn't work like that . . ."

The half-breed had turned the key in the lock and started to pull open the door. Then saw through the crack of its first opening the dim light from a gas mantle glinting on something metallic. And he chose counterat-

117

tack rather than defense—jerking the door wide instead of slamming it closed.

"Down!" he roared at the newspaperman, who had powered up from the swivel chair as he started to vent his anger. And went down himself, into a balanced crouch as he drew the Remington smoothly from its holster.

The blond haired kid with crooked teeth expressed terror as the initiative was snatched from him. Instead of being faced with an unready target framed in the doorway he saw the blur of the half-breed's moving form and the fear frozen newspaperman standing like a carved statue in front of the swivel-chair across the room. Panic caused the twitch of his finger which squeezed the trigger as he tried to lower the aim of the Frontier Colt toward Edge.

The exploded bullet cracked across the top of the half-breed's shoulder and ricocheted off the metal castor of the dilapidated leather-covered chair, its trajectory altered from a downward to an upward flight by striking the curved surface. And was finally stopped by the tissue at the nape of Dickens' neck after tunnelling into his throat and severing his windpipe.

The newspaperman coughed, the sound like a polite gesture of interruption, died on his feet and dropped back into the swivel-chair.

By then a second gunshot had cracked out, from the upward angled barrel of the Remington. This bullet did not require a deflection and drove deep into its intended target—entering low down in the youngster's belly and destroying countless lengths of intestines before it came to rest lodged against a rib.

"Oh, shit," the young killer murmured as he dropped his gun and staggered backwards, clutching at the dark stain which was blossoming on the front of his pants between the flaps of his open topcoat.

"As a hired gun you're one heap of that, kid," Edge rasped through clenched teeth as he came erect and snatched a glance over his shoulder.

The chair had made a half turn as the dead weight fell into it, so that the newspaperman's body was toward the desk now. But his head was hung over the low back of the chair, his upside-down face visible from the doorway. Blood trickled at each side of his neck and dripped steadily to the floor. The eyes were wide and staring, seemed to direct toward the half-breed the accusing glare of a man betrayed.

"Yeah, feller," Edge murmured in a forceful whisper. "I'm wrong. You're dead right."

Rod Kirkby had come to a halt with his back to the door of the apartment across the landing. He had started to slide down it, but managed to prevent the move. Now stood with his knees bent and thighs splayed, hands still clawed at the base of his belly. He held his head up, his terror-filled eyes fixed upon the face of Edge, which looked satanic in the dim glow from the gas mantel and against the brighter light in the apartment behind.

"You're going to die, kid," the half-breed announced harshly.

Kirkby swallowed hard. But not all the saliva in his mouth. Some spilled out over his trembling lower lip and ran down his chin. "I know it," he croaked.

"Confession is good for the soul." He stepped up close to the injured youngster and gripped the lapels of the open topcoat with his left hand while his right pressed the muzzle of the Remington tight against the pulsing temple.

"What else can you do to me, mister?" Kirkby said, and managed to get a note of defiance into his voice.

"Make it quick. Like you were a horse with no hope.

119

Feller can take a long time to die with a bullet in his belly."

Up close—over a range of no more than six inches—the lean face did not look so evil to the dying man. It was devoid of all emotion, good or bad. So Kirkby experienced shock for a moment before agony as the half-breed kneed him viciously in the crotch. He screamed once, then again. First in reaction to the searing pain in his genitals. Then to the greater agony as his body jerked involuntarily and the movement tore the merciful veneer of numbness off the bullet wound.

The high-pitched sounds caused one of the mumbling voices beyond the apartment door to roar: "What's goin' on out there?"

"Stay out of my business!" Edge snarled, and lowered his voice. "Long and painful. A bullet in the brain and it'll all be over."

Sweat and saliva was streaming down Kirkby's chin now. When he tried to say something only a gurlging sound issued from his mouth.

"Who sent you, kid?"

"The boss." The two words were like tiny scratches on the silence.

"Orlando?"

Kirkby shook his head. "Him the first time. At . . . at the . . . ho . . . hotel This time . . . Boss . . . Marlon. Jesus it's . . . like my . . . insides are burnin' up."

"He still at his house?"

A deep swallow and then a shake of the head. "No. No, he's at the . . . the Silver Lady."

"Obliged, kid."

Edge clicked back the hammer of the revolver.

Kirkby sucked in a deep breath to power out words without pauses between them. "Please, mister! I don't wanna die! I told you what you wanted! Hopin' you wouldn't kill me! I'll take the pain for a chance to live."

The half-breed eased the muzzle of the Remington away from the temple of the youngster and the pain contorted features of the doomed Kirkby were briefly altered by a wan smile of relief. Then the gun cracked out its killing shot, the bullet smashing into the head on the left and exploding out from the right amid a welter of blood, pulped tissue and bone shards.

As Edge released his hold on the coat lapels and the corpse crumpled to the floor the man behind the door ignored the pleas of a distraught woman and yelled, "You murderin' sonofabitch!"

The half-breed cast a final glance in through the open doorway of Mason Dickens' apartment. Then scowled down at the corpse of Rod Kirkby. "He ain't in no condition to start an argument about that, feller," he called to the frightened and angry man who had snarled the accusation "On account of I just give him the kind that went in one ear and out the other."

Chapter Ten

DOORS on the lower landings which had been opened by the nervously curious after the first two gunshots were hurriedly slammed closed at Edge's footfalls were heard on the stairways. Then were re-opened more cautiously after he had passed. Out on Delancy Street the only living thing in sight was a gray stallion hitched to the iron railings which guarded the basement entry to the apartment building. More lighted windows showed in the façade of this building, those flanking it and those directly across the street than when the half-breed had arrived. But as he raked his now expressionless eyes over his surroundings, the watchers ducked into the cover of solid walls. Only dared to show themselves at the windows again when they heard the clop of shod hooves on the paved street surface diminish as the tall, lean, western-attired stranger rode a dead man's horse to the corner and headed north, deliberately extracting empty shells from his revolver and sliding fresh bullets into the chambers of the cylinder.

He rode the city streets as he would ride the trails of mountains or plains apparently at ease but actually poised on the very verge of whiplash reaction, every muscle in his powerful body tensed to respond should his constantly moving eyes spot a sign of potential danger. And thus as he rode across now-deserted late-night streets and along empty avenues, his attitude gave no hint of the burning anger and massive hatred which lurked deep inside him.

To anyone who happened to glance out of one of the thousands of windows in the hundreds of tall buildings, he would look like nothing more than a weary, un-washed, unshaven and oddly-dressed-for-the-city man riding easily toward a destination he was in no hurry to reach.

The glinting eyes that swung to and fro between the narrowed lids searched for the unknown agents of iden-tifiable enemies. Gilpatrick's officers who Dickens had said were looking for him. The hired guns of Marlon and Orlando who might be guarding against the eventu-ality that Rod Kirkby had failed again. Boss Black's men because there was a chance the Negro could feel he had been double-crossed. And government men because Lincoln might consider that, outside his control, the half-breed was capable of doing more harm than good.

But he saw no one on the ride from Delancy Street to the Silver Lady Bar between 54th and 55th on Park. He found his way there easily, for this city he had grown to hate and had one thing going for it—the numbering rather than naming of most of the streets and avenues enabled a stranger to find his way about without diffi-culty.

After he had dismounted a block down from the pool of gaslight that illuminated the whorehouse sign and started to walk north, a drizzling rain began to fall. And several nearby clocks struck the single note to mark the time as one in the morning. He pulled his hat lower down over his brow and turned up the collar of his top-coat. He did not have to check that the right side of the coat was rucked up, allowing his hand easy access to the butt of the Remington jutting from the holster.

Directly across the avenue from the whorehouse a new building was in the course of erection. The bricks were laid to second-story level, but without frames or glasses in the windows yet. Above this was the skeleton framework of iron girders rising to the seventh story. Many long ladders zig-zagged up through the vertical girders to reach the horizontal ones.

When Edge had come to the whorehouse earlier, men had still been working on the building and the cement they had been laying was not yet dry. The smell of it was strong in the rain washed air as he turned off the sidewalk and started down the steps to the basement entrance of the Silver Lady Bar. Light filtered out through the colored panes of circular glass in the swing doors. He could hear no noise from beyond. Certainly nobody was playing the piano now. He pushed open the doors like they were batwings at the entrance to a frontier town saloon and stepped across the threshold, right hand close to the butt of the revolver but not touching it.

Some twenty men were doing more than merely touching their guns. They had their hands fisted around the butts of cocked Frontier Colts, aiming the short-barrel revolvers at Edge as the half-breed came to a halt on the threshold, the doors held half open by his broad shoulders. Young men, well dressed in city suits, clean and well-groomed.

Mario and Rico were as smartly turned out as the rest of the Italian looking gunmen. Perhaps expressed a little more blatantly their wish to sending a killing shot toward the newcomer.

"I told you!" Luigi Orlando blurted. "He's with Boss Black!"

The men with the guns were aligned along each side of the room, in front of the booths which now had their drapes drawn aside. Orlando, who had a large, dark swelling on his temple where he had crashed into the wall at the Staten Island mansion, stood with his back to the circular bar. His godfather was also back to the bar, but he was sitting on a stool. Both men were still attired in full evening dress. The obscene fountain was as silent as the deserted piano.

"Is Luigi correct, cowboy?" the older man asked, his expression and tone of voice cold and hard.

"I'm with me," Edge answered, not allowing his curiosity about the massive turnout of gunmen to show.

"Then why are you here at precisely the time which Black arranged for my meet with him?"

Doubt filled the half-breed's mind. It did not smother the anger and hatred which Mason Dickens' death had aroused in him. But it did give him pause for thought, to wonder if his instinctive desire to kill was directed toward the wrong man.

"Guess it ain't a coincidence, feller," he answered softly. He nodded at Orlando. "His boy Kirkby just tried to kill me again."

Marlon clenched his fists and looked as angry as when he had shattered the brandy balloon at his mansion on Staten Island. His dark eyes moved in their sockets to direct his displeasure toward Rico and Mario. Both men sensed this and were suddenly anxious as they were drawn to shift their attention away from the half-breed.

"We did as you asked, Mr. Marlon," Rico said quickly, nervously.

Mario nodded the truth of this. "I told Kirkby your orders, Mr. Marlon." His face abruptly lit up. "You can ask Miss Fay! She was right here when I spoke to him."

Some of the strain left Marlon as he looked back at Edge. "I am a man of my word, cowboy. I am also a man who insists his orders are obeyed. Rico and Mario used one of my private boats to cross to the city ahead of you and ensure that Luigi's men were aware of my orders. You have heard . . ."

"Uncle!" Orlando cut in. "You don't have to give explanations to him! We're wasting time! It's a trick. It has to be!"

"A trick?" the older man posed. "To gain what end, my boy? Your men are still on guard upstairs are they not? Will warn us if others approach the building?"

Edge had to believe what Marlon said. The man had kept his word. And Rico and Mario had done as they were ordered. So the only lie told was by Kirkby. Why?

"Think about it, cowboy," Marlon went on, his soft-spoken response to his godson having eased Orlando's mind. "If I wanted you dead, you would have more than twenty bullets in your corpse by now."

He gestured with both hands to encompass the silent, grim-faced gunmen lining each side of the room.

"I am thinking, feller."

"That Luigi is right? A trick had been played. But on you."

A rifle shot sounded out on the street. The crack of the explosion almost masked by the shattering of the window in the door held open by the half-breed's right shoulder. The bullet drilled through the carpet to bury itself in the floor. A thousand glinting-shards of multi-colored glass showered across in front of Edge's chest. As curses ripped from the mouths of the gunmen and Orlando, the men instinctively dropping down into crouches, their eyes raked toward Marlon.

Edge was already looking at the man. Saw, a split-second before anyone else, the expression of depthless rage take command of every line on the face. And knew there was no time to wait for him to give an order. For the half-breed could not read the mind behind the glaring eyes, had no way of knowing what words would issue through the clenched teeth between the snarling lips.

So Edge had to assume the worse. And he threw himself backwards and to the side. Out of the doorway and onto the hard, wet cement at the foot of the steps.

The doors swung closed. Then were forced partially open again by a hail of bullets that cracked through the drizzling rain to slam into them, exploding splinters of wood and shattering the other glass panel.

"Kill him!" Emilio Marlon shrieked rage driving his voice to a high pitch. "Kill the *bastardo!*"

More than twenty revolvers were fired, to pepper the inside of the doors with bullets. None of them penetrated the stout timber. Two cracked through the broken windows to dig chips of cement from the wall below the railings.

But Edge was out of the line of fire anyway, bellying up the stone steps with the Remington in his right hand. His mind was racing in search of an explanation and this aroused a self-anger that was even more powerful than the rage he felt toward an unknown enemy. Because right now, when he was caught in the crossfire between opposing groups of gunmen, an explanation was unimportant. All that mattered was to get completely out of the line of fire.

More gunshots exploded as he forced his mind away from its irrelevant line of thought. From inside the Silver Lady Bar. From the half-finished building across the street and from the front rooms of the whorehouse above him. Men were yelling and cursing. And some women were screaming. The lightly falling rain acted to make the stench of drifting gunsmoke more pungent. Then a faint odor of escaping gas started to permeate the air as bullets shattered the lamps which illuminated the bar sign above the riddled doors.

But the street lights continued to gleam through the

mist-like rain—showing up Edge as a clear target as he lunged from the steps and sprinted along the sidewalk. Bullets ricocheted off the cement under his thudding feet and exploded chips of stone from the façade of the building. One such chip inscribed an inch long cut in his cheek just as he powered into a turn that took him into the inky darkness of the alley at the side of the building under attack. A final volley of rifle shots was directed into the mouth of the alley before the men across the street returned their full attention back to the building.

Edge slowed from his headlong run, still stooped as the ricocheting bullets and flying chips of dislodged stone spat and hissed around his head. He was breathing fast, more from the tension of fear than because of the exertion. He had to struggle to keep his anger an ice-cold ball in the pit of his stomach, prevent it from expanding to engulf his entire being and becoming white-hot.

Somebody had used him. And got two men killed in the process. Kirkby didn t matter. He was owed what he got from the half-breed. But Mason Dickens, he was different. Another innocent victim, like the tobacco grower from Carolina, of the violence that dogged Edge. But why had he been used? Who had sent Kirkby after him—had enough influence over the gunman to persuade him to disobey Boss Marlon's orders and then lie with virtually his dying breath?

"You just can't keep out of trouble, can you?"

Edge had come to a stop and was waiting for his eyes to adjust to the darkness. Was inwardly cursing himself as his mind involuntarily returned to the futile search for answers that even if they were found would serve no useful purpose here and now. He heard Lincoln's voice during a brief lull in the gun battle. And did not recognize it as the government man's before he swung the

Remington to aim in the direction from which the words came.

"It trails me almost as close as you do, feller," the half-breed rasped as the short, fat, balding man stepped away from a doorway recessed into the side of the building across the alley from the whorehouse. He still held the cardboard suitcase in one hand. In the other was a Frontier Colt loosely gripped and hanging down at his side so that it was aimed at the ground.

"But you always stay one jump ahead of it, don't you? Far enough away to survive."

The shooting and the shouting had started up again but within the confining high walls of the buildings flanking the alley the sounds had a distant ring to them. So that the two men, standing six feet apart, could talk at a normal conversational level and still hear each other.

"Mason Dickens didn't survive," Edge said, as calm now as his tone of voice. His Remington was still aimed at the bulging belly of Lincoln. His narrow eyes beneath the hooded lids had now adjusted to the dark of the alley and he was able to see the dough-colored face of the man. It expressed what seemed to be a frown of genuine sadness.

"What happened?" He spoke with regret.

"Don't you know, feller?"

"I can't be in two places at one time, Mr. Edge. By the way."

"Yeah?"

"If you fire that gun at me, I'll have your company in hell."

He tipped back his head to look up at the strip of rain clouds visible between the high walls. Two men were leaning over the roof of the building behind Lincoln and as Edge looked up at them they thrust rifles out, showing them briefly against the sky before they resumed their aim down into the alley.

The half-breed pursed his lips as he looked at Lincoln, then drew back his gun hand and slid the revolver into its holster, easing the hammer to the rest. "Guess I can wait."

"Why don't you do that? At Grand Central. For the train west. You can use some time counting this." He lowered the suitcase to the ground and nudged it toward the half-breed with the toe of his boot.

"Money?"

"What else? Of course, the case isn't full of it. Just five thousand. For you to keep your mouth shut."

"About what?"

"Uncle Sam's involvement in this." He waved his now empty left hand toward the Park Avenue end of the alley where the acrid smelling gunsmoke could now be seen drifting in thick billows through the rain under the street lights.

"How much did you pay Kirkby for shutting up the newspaperman, feller?"

"That wasn't supposed to happen, Mr. Edge!" Lincoln was not sad anymore. He sounded irritated. And there was a scowl on his pale face.

"I know, but it did."

"What was Dickens to you?" Lincoln snapped.

"The only feller in this city who made me an offer I could refuse without the risk of getting my head blown off."

The government man thought about this for a few moments against the background sounds of gunfire. Then he nodded. "All right, Mr. Edge, I guess I can understand how you feel. But don't you owe me something, too? I didn't have to come out into the open and give you the money. I could have stayed back in cover

130

and saved five thousand dollars of taxpayers' money. And you would never have known I sent Kirkby after you."

"I'd have figured it out, feller," the half-breed countered. "When I gave myself time to think. Remembered that you were some place close down at the ferry landing when I gave the cab driver Dickens' address. And that only somebody like you would have to pull to keep the law off my back. Dickens told me every police officer in the city was looking for me after what happened the last time I went to the Silver Lady Bar. And I figured I'm an easy man to see in a town like this."

Lincoln nodded again and now he seemed to be growing impatient. "All right, all right. But it doesn't matter anymore. What's done is done. And the only thing that's gone wrong is Dickens getting killed. If he's got any dependents the government will take care of them. And he died in a good cause. With Marlon dead his bunch won't last much longer and Boss Black'll have the city sewn up for himself. Not the way decent people would like things to be, but a whole lot better than having two gangs fighting over it all the time."

"Something else went wrong," Edge said evenly. "I didn't kill the old man."

"You didn't . . .?" Lincoln choked on the words he was rasping.

Two shots cracked out, isolated by distance from the gunfire being exchanged across the streets. Immediately overhead. And two rifles fell through the rain washed air to clatter to the ground at either side of where Edge and Lincoln stood. The two men tipped back their heads to peer upwards. And saw that the owners of the rifles were hanging over the rim of the roof, heads inert between their slightly swinging arms.

The half-breed drew, cocked and leveled the Remington. And the click of the hammer overlaid Lincoln's expression of shock with one of fear as he looked again at Edge.

"Do not kill him yet, cowboy," Emilio Marlon growled from a second-story window of the whorehouse.

Lincoln had snatched his terror-filled eyes away from the half-breed's scowling face when he heard the window slide up in its frame. To stare at the man who gave the order.

Edge glanced upwards again, too. But not to look at Marlon. Instead to see if the men who had shot the government agents from the whorehouse roof were now in a position to back their boss's play. They were not. It was impossible to check all the windows in the side of the building. Because it was too dark and there was not the time, between choosing his course of action and putting it into effect.

He turned from the waist, tipped back his head and swung his gun hand around and up. Saw the satisfied smirk on Marlon's face begin to change into a frown of rage. Saw also the fingers of the man hooked over the window sill tighten as he prepared to push himself backwards into the room. Then glimpsed, before he snatched his glinting eyed gaze away, the small hole in the center of Emilio's forehead as the bullet from the Remington found its mark.

"Uncle!" Luigi Orlando shrieked from out of the darkened room into which the dead man was flipped by the impact of the bullet.

"Move it!" Edge snarled at Lincoln, who seemed to be rooted to the ground by the shock of what had just happened. Then he clutched at the government man's upper arm, forced him in a half turn and shoved him along the alley. Away from Park Avenue with its lights, muzzle flashes, gunsmoke, shouts, screams and constant barrage of shots.

"You're crazy, you know that!" the government man yelled, plunging out of shock and into elation, racing forward, leading the half-breed around a sharp turn heading for the lights of 55th Street. At the mouth of the alley he halted, gasping for breath and needing to lean against the wall. "I was sure you were going to kill me back there," he forced out. "Why . . .?"

"Figure to be on the winning side, feller," Edge cut in, peering back down the alley, then checking the lengths of 55th Street stretching away into the misty rain in each direction.

Lincoln showed his teeth beneath the bushy red mustache in a broad grin. "I'd say you're a man who always is."

Edge started along 55th toward the intersection with Park. "Not always," he growled.

"But you're sure to be this time," the government man said excitedly as he hurried to catch up with the half-breed. "Like I told you before, with Marlon dead they're finished.".

Edge spat a globule of saliva out over the sidewalk and into the gutter. "Yeah, I already heard one of them yell uncle."

Chapter Eleven

As HE looked across the broad width of Park Avenue with Lincoln standing at his side, the half-breed witnessed another example of how New York was much like a frontier town but on a larger scale. For the gun battle had become a spectacle for the citizens who lived in the immediate locality. There were upwards of two hundred men, women and children on the avenue to the north of where the gangs of Boss Black and the now dead Emilio Marlon were trading a constant barrage of rifle and revolver fire. And the crowd was swelling by the moment as the excitedly curious from farther away came running, riding horseback or aboard wagons and carriages. And there were just as many people to the south of the battle arena, both eager crowds held back beyond points of relative safety by lines of scowling and cursing police officers.

Out west the crowds would not have been so large and there would not have been so many lawmen. They were the only differences. The attraction was precisely the same. Men were trying to kill each other—were killing each other—and such violence was a big draw.

Like the First Battle of Bull Run. The man called Edge had been there, too.

He and Lincoln reached the far side of Park Avenue after elbowing and shouldering their way through the press of people who scowled and snarled at the men who momentarily blocked their view. And the half-breed put thoughts of the past out of his mind.

"Where we going?" the government man wanted to know, breathless again after the struggle to force a way through the crowd.

"I figure to even a score," Edge rasped as he quickened his pace now that he was free of the rubbernecks. And used alleyways again to reach the rear of the partially constructed building where Black's men were positioned.

Lincoln tried to voice his objections as soon as he realized where the tall, lean, impassive-faced man was headed. But Edge always stayed in front, obviously not listening to the fast-spoken, anxious words. And then, as they drew closer to the half-breed's objective, the volume of gunfire got louder and Lincoln gave up his attempts. Even considered turning away and hurrying off into the rain-filled darkness, leaving the westerner to get himself killed if that was what he wanted. But Lincoln did not do this. And was not sure why until the question was posed, totally unexpectedly, as Edge came to a halt at a glassless rear window of the building under construction.

"You got a reason for tagging after me, feller?"

The half-breed had paused to eject the empty shell case from the Remington's cylinder and replace it with a fresh bullet from his gunbelt.

Lincoln replied without having to think about it. "You could have killed me, Edge!" he yelled above the gunfire. It was much louder on this side of the avenue. For Black's men were using rifles, their cracks resounding within the bare stone walls of the roofless shell of the building in the making. "But you didn't."

"You don't owe me a thing!" the half-breed yelled as he swung a leg up and over the window sill.

"Surely you want an explanation?"

"All I want is out of this," Edge replied, but he spoke without shouting, and with his back to Lincoln as he drew his other leg over the sill and advanced closer to the center of the battle.

He spoke the truth. The same kind of truth he had traded with Emilio Marlon. There was only one kind and Edge tried to live by it. But it was not always possible. Not when other people messed with his business and he was forced to admit they had right on their side.

It didn't happen often because for most of the time Edge did not give a shit about the difference between right and wrong, not when his life was on the line.

The last time it had happened was in the War Between the States, when he wore a uniform which bound him to the cause of the Union. That bloody period in his life had been one long series of compromises between his personal views of right and wrong, truth and lies.

And now he was caught up in a similar situation. More complex, perhaps, since this was a three-way war. Between Emilio Marlon and Boss Black, with the U.S. government—the Union—determined to drive both factions into retreat.

There was no uniform on his powerful frame now. No captain's insignia on his shoulders and hats. No measly army pay to buy his allegiance. Just a sudden realization, which almost hit him too late, that the amoral, conniving government man with the illustrious name had right on his side.

And in that instant Edge had broken his word. Gunned down Emilio Marlon—a man he admired and for whom he felt an affinity—rather than put a bullet into Lincoln. Just as, many years previously, it had been necessary to kill countless fine men simply because they wore uniforms of Confederate gray. When all the time the half-breed knew of at least six Union troopers who were more deserving of bullets.

There were no men at the rear of the building, so Edge was able to climb to an elevated vantage point without being seen, in danger only from stray bullets that cracked out from the many broken windows in the façade of the whorehouse to find lucky entrance to this building through windows with no glass to shatter. He climbed up ladders which bowed under his weight, each of them lashed securely to iron girders which would eventually support the floors and ceilings of upper storys. The walls to partition the rooms of the first and second floor of the building were already in place and it was these which provided cover for the half-breed as he ascended the steeply pitched ladders.

Then he was above their level, crouched on a girder at the rear of the building, unprotected from the drizzle which soaked his clothes and formed pools on his hat brim to drip down in front of his face. Temporarily away from the danger of the occasional bullet which not only found its way in through a front window but also hissed between the gaps which formed interior doorways. Most of the bullets had not made it that far. Fired wildly and blindly, angrily and fearfully, they deformed themselves against the façade of the building and lodged in the stonework or drooped to the sidewalk. But a few which did gain entrance found human targets and when he had been down at first-floor level, Edge had heard the screams and groans and curses of the wounded and dying, these sounds of human suffering counterpointing the constant barrage of rifle and revolver fire. Up here amid the falling rain and the rising gunsmoke only the loudest sounds could be heard.

He interrupted his climbing and instead moved forward, in a crouch at first and then down on his belly as he neared the front of the building, glancing across the street at the façade of the whorehouse but mostly peering downward to either side of the girder atop the dividing walls on which he was balanced. Then he climbed again, up another bowing ladder to the third floor level. And cursed softly when he discovered he had to go up to the fourth floor—only then was able to see over the dividing walls into every front-facing room of the building. Five of them, two rooms proper to either side of the entrance hall. Occupied by up to forty men, most of them either blasting out through the windows with Winchester repeaters or crouched down in the process of reloading. Seven were out of the fight, sprawled on the cement floor, two of these gripped by the inertness of death, the other five agonizingly conscious of their blood-spurting wounds.

Edge's narrowed, glinting eyes located the man he had come here to kill and then glanced again across Park Avenue. Behind the bullet-pocked façade of the whorehouse there would be similar scenes in each room. Dead and wounded on the floors, while at each shattered window the survivors would empty their guns toward the unseen enemy and then withdraw to reload as other men continued the gunfire.

But it would not go on like this for much longer. Eventually one group of gunmen would run out of ammunition and their opposition would move in for the kill. Or perhaps patience would be expended before bullets and a decision would be taken for a reckless advance across the avenue. Certainly it was too late now for anything more subtle than this, as the half-breed could see as he lengthened the focus of his hooded eyes and raked them over the surrounding rooftops. For there were men crouched at chimney stacks and behind signs and low walls at the eaves. Men with rifles, the wet barrels of which did not gleam so brightly as the polished buttons on their uniform tunics. Municipal policemen who watched and waited for the right time to mop up what was left of the opposing factions. In positions where they could prevent any attempt at flanking moves by either Black's or Marlon's men. Perfectly placed to contain the raucous gun battle to the whorehouse and the partially finished building.

"Now you can see why the law didn't bother with you, Edge," Lincoln said, breathless again after his exertion of climbing the ladders.

The sound of the familiar voice did not surprise the half-breed this time, for he had been aware of the government man's cautious progress up to the fourth floor and then Lincoln's slow crawl out along the girders to the point where he now lay, six feet away from where Edge was squatting on his haunches.

"They had bigger fish to fry."

"First they had to get them in the net, feller. And I was the bait, uh?"

"Thought you would fire the first shot, Mr. Edge," Lincoln answered, his expression mournful again. "After you made your deal with Marlon at his house I had to think of something else. You see, there's a kind of unwritten code between Black and Marlon. Their men kill each other all the time. But the Bosses themselves, they're immune to that kind of thing. But if one of them were to get killed and it looked like the other one gave the order. Well . . ."

He waved a hand to indicate the battle that was being fought below his high perch.

"I didn't fire the first shot," Edge reminded, looking down to where Boss Black stood in the cover of a stout wall, smoking a cigar and apparently content with the way the fight was going.

Lincoln moved up off his belly to straddle the girder, his legs dangling in the air each side.

"I set up the meet. Used two of my own men who'd infiltrated the groups. Both Black and Marlon thought it was on the level, but being the kind of men they are, I knew they'd be suspicious of each other's motives. But it would all have fizzled out to nothing if you hadn't shown up, Mr. Edge."

"Kirkby?"

"Used my man who was in Marlon's group. Had him tell Kirkby that Marlon really did want you killed. A private job. Very secret because the old man didn't want it known he'd broken his word of honor. These Italian people are very strong on the honor thing."

"Not like Uncle Sam."

"Ends justify means," Lincoln replied simply.

"You had me covered in case Kirkby got the drop on me?"

The government man smiled wanly. And shook his head. "You're a born survivor, Mr. Edge. I knew you'd be able to handle Kirkby. And you did. And then you did exactly what I thought you'd do. Came hell for leather after Marlon. Because that's your way. But then you got to talking with him again. Instead of doing what I thought you would."

"Nobody knows anybody else completely, feller."

A nod of agreement. "But as it turned out, it didn't matter. You showing up made Marlon more nervous than ever. And it had the same effect on Black and his men. One of them got nervous enough to fire the first shot."

"Which might have happened anyway," the half-breed muttered sourly. "Without Dickens getting killed and me having to kill Kirkby. Hell, feller, you could have climbed up here and thrown some lead across the street yourself."

Another nod of agreement. Accompanied by the familiar expression of regret. "You're right. What can I say?"

"Just that it seemed like a good idea at the time."

"Sure. That can cover a lot of mistakes."

"We all make them."

There was a long silence on the high girder as the two men perched upon it looked down at the scene of the battle. The intensity of the shooting had eased now and Edge guessed that a tactical change was about to take place. Shots were still being exchanged, but it was as if the men behind the guns had lost their enthusiasm for what they were doing. If they hit a human target, they did not have the satisfaction of seeing their opponent fall, nor even hearing his vocal response to having lead tearing into his flesh. All they could see was the damage they were doing to the buildings housing their enemies. And hear gunshots and the sounds of bullets impacting futilely against unfeeling stone and brick.

Then, with a shocking suddenness, all shooting ceased and for perhaps two stretched seconds there was complete silence clamped down over this area of the city. Not even a single sound invaded this stillness from a distance, as if the softly falling, mist-like rain acted as a solid barrier to such intrusions.

"Black!"

It was Luigi Orlando who yelled the name of the obese Negro boss. And his shout caused a mumbling of talk to sound among the two crowds of police-controlled watchers.

The cigar-smoking fat man advanced across the hallway toward the front door. Sheldon and another man moved to flank him. None of the three showed themselves in the opening.

"What do you want, punk?" Black shouted, having to take the cigar from between his teeth to give his voice volume.

141

"Talk!"

"I don't talk with the monkey, punk! Only the organ grinder!"

"My godfather's dead! Murdered by that sneaky bastard calls himself Edge!"

There was a ripple of talk among Black's men. Which was immediately curtailed when the Negro rasped an order that was passed from room to room.

"That mean you're the boss now?"

"Yeah. And what we're doing is stupid!"

"What you wanna do instead, punk?"

"Have another meet! A proper one! Not like this! We were tricked! You and us! By that Edge bastard!"

Black was talking at the same time as Orlando. But only for the ears of Sheldon and the other man who was close to him. And when he was through, these two withdrew to pass on what they had heard.

"What do you say, Black?" Orlando demanded.

"You're talkin', punk! I'm listenin'!"

"Look, there has to be half the city law out on the street! Waitin' for us to kill each other! You and your men leave! And we'll fix a meet. Face to face! Man to man!"

"The man's dead, punk! Just leaves you! And I got nothin' I want to talk to a punk about!"

"Black, listen!" Orlando's confidence had gradually been ebbing as the Negro shouted answers he did not want to hear. Now the Italian sounded close to panic.

And the overweight Negro was smart enough to guess at the reason for this. He nodded to Sheldon, who aimed his Winchester into the air and squeezed the trigger. Perhaps saw Edge and Lincoln silhouetted against the cloudy sky just as he fired the shot. Or perhaps not until a split second afterwards. But certainly the weakly handsome expert knife thrower did not have time to alter the direction of the shot and make it more than a signal that was exploded from its muzzle.

Black's men poured out of the building through the doorway and the glassless windows. Across the sidewalk and over the avenue, blasting covering fire at the whorehouse and trusting the Negro's judgment that Luigi Orlando wanted the truce because his men were out of ammunition.

Sheldon shouted a warning against the bedlam of noise from rifles and throats, but only Black was close enough to hear it. Both men gazed up at the half-breed and Lincoln, and Sheldon pumped the lever action of his rifle.

But the man who was so skilled with a knife was not fast enough with the Winchester. Edge had drawn the Remington, cocked the hammer and squeezed the trigger before Sheldon had completed jacking a shell into the rifle's breech.

The revolver bullet drilled into the center of the forehead of the upturned face—a perfect match for the wound which had ended the life of Emilio Marlon.

As the man collapsed into a heap on the floor, Black looked desperately around him, swinging his body from the waist, searching for a weapon or a means of escape.

"The Bosses are never armed!" Lincoln yelled at Edge as the half-breed's thumb cocked the hammer back and the cylinder clicked round.

It was escape the Negro had been seeking. Now that he saw none was possible, he spread his arms to the side, hands splayed. As if he had heard the government man's comment and was showing proof of it.

"They got a lot of sonsofbitches working for them," the half-breed answered. "Men like that don't need to do the barking and biting themselves."

Black had miscalculated the abilities of the godson who had inherited the empire of the godfather. Orlando had been putting on an act of fear—to draw the opposition out into the open and within effective range of his men's revolvers. For, just as the men with the more powerful rifles reached the sidewalk in front of the whorehouse, death was rained down upon them. As, from every window in the front of the building, men who had been holding fire thrust out their short barrel Frontier Colts and fanned the hammers.

Half of Black's men fell onto the sidewalk and into the gutter, blood gushing from wounds in heads, bodies and limbs. The rest turned to run, but there was no cover within reach and they were back shot, to pitch and roll on the paved surface of Park Avenue. Any of them who revealed he was merely wounded by screaming his agony or writhing to try to ease the pain, drew a barrage of fire that instantly silenced and stilled him.

While Edge's attention was apparently distracted by the brutal slaughter out on the street, Boss Black thought he saw a chance to escape. And he moved into a waddling run through the bleak shells which would one day be rooms of the completed building. Heading for the rear.

The half-breed was aware of the Negro's retreat, but it was Lincoln who shot the running fat man. It needed two bullets to bring the boss down. Both in the back. After the first one, he was still able to stagger a few steps, out of one room and into another. The second knocked him down onto his face and the weight of his falling body caused something like clods of thick mud to spray up on either side. He lay utterly still.

The killing shots had been lost amid the final barrage of gunfire from the whorehouse across the street. Moments before another solid silence dropped, blanket-like, over the scene of the Park Avenue battle. To be broken by shouts across the surrounding rooftops as the uniformed lawmen with rifles were ordered to climb down and move in. The police officers already on the avenue had to struggle harder to hold back the crowds of watchers who grew more anxious to indulge their ghoulish curiosity at close quarters.

"You had a reason for doing that, feller?" Edge asked, his tone hard and his eyes ice-cold.

"The law wouldn't have shot him. He's paid too much to too many of them. They'd have arrested him and he'd have been out of gaol by morning. Same as that bunch across the street will be. There won't be a firearm in sight when the police go in there. The dead will get the blame. Lawyers will claim the rest of them were just innocent clients of the whores." Lincoln's expression and voice were mournful. "Black's lawyers can't help him now. I had to make sure of that."

"He was mine," the half-breed rasped, exploring with fingertips the dried blood on the cut across his cheek. "Even up what I did to Marlon. A lousy deal for both of them, but you made it the only one I could make."

"Did it for you, too," Lincoln said as he started to inch gingerly back along the girder toward the top of the nearest ladder. "You didn't know about Marlon not carrying a gun. I told you about Black. Way things turned out, you'd have had to shoot an unarmed man in the back. That's not the western way, is it?"

"East or west, don't make any difference to me, feller," Edge replied as he started down the ladder in the wake of the government man. "You have to kill somebody, you do it. Men who live by that code crap only wind up dying by it."

There was no more talk until they had reached ground level.

"What does it matter who killed him?" Lincoln asked. "So long as he's dead. Orlando got smart for once so him and his Italians get to have the city for themselves. Like I said before, not the way decent people would wish but we're stuck with the situation."

"Decent people like us?" Edge growled.

Lincoln sighed wearily. "So I put it badly. To hell with it. Just don't murder anyone else in Kansas and you won't die by the rope there. Better deal than the one I made you make with Marlon and Black. And the money's still in the alley across the street if you want it."

"Obliged for the amnesty. Government can keep the blood money."

"Suit yourself."

"Usually do." He had been rolling a cigarette. Now he lit it. "Ain't always possible though."

"One thing, Mr. Edge."

"Yeah?" the half-breed asked as he made to move from one empty shell of a room through the doorless gap into another.

"Best you don't come back to New York. Orlando will be gunning for you for shooting his godfather. And Gilpatrick will be back in the hunt now his team came out the winners."

Edge nodded. "Staying away from this town won't be any hardship."

"Can understand why you'll have no regrets."

"Just two."

"Two?"

"Named Rico and Mario. If they're still alive after the shoot out. Twice they pointed guns at me after I warned them not to. Never did kill them for that."

Lincoln followed him through the gap and bumped into him as he halted, became aware that, like the half-breed, he was sinking to his ankles in the rain-softened, freshly laid floor. It was in the center of this room that

146

Boss Black had died, his obese form slumped face down and half submerged in the cement.

"Guess I'd better have them haul him out of there," the government man muttered as he backed out through the doorway and the half-breed followed him.

"Why not leave him there, feller?" Edge answered, rasping the back of a hand over his bristled jaw under the cigarette that drooped from a corner of his thin-lipped mouth. "Few hours after the rain lets up, decent people of this city'll be able to see an example of the kind of bastard the law allows to stink up their streets."

Lincoln blinked his confusion. "You lost me, Mr. Edge."

The half-breed shot a baleful glance at the deceptively innocuous-looking Lincoln, then gestured with a careless wave of his brown-skinned hand toward the corpse sprawled in the soft, wet cement. "A hardened criminal."

SPECIAL PREVIEW

The blazing Western series by the author of the bestselling EDGE series

George G. Gilman

The adventures of Adam Steele are written by the author of our bestselling Edge series, who has created another brand of blazing Westerns to show the way it really was in the West . . . a grim and gritty view unpolished by history, untamed by time!

Outraged over his father's murder, Adam Steele rides to his destiny on a bloody trail of revenge and retribution. He carries with him a rifle bearing the dedication that is his inspiration: "To Benjamin P. Steele, with gratitude, Abraham Lincoln." And Steele won't stop until he finds his father's killers . . . and any other killer who crosses his path!

The following is an edited version of the first few chapters, as we are introduced to Adam Steele*:

Adam Steele reined his bay gelding to a halt at the crest of a rise and split his mouth in a gentle smile as he surveyed the lights of the city spread before him. It had been a long ride from Richmond and he spent a few relaxed moments in quiet contemplation of the end of the journey. Then he sighed and heeled the horse forward down the gentle incline that led into Washington.

He rode upright, but not tall in the Western saddle. He was just a shade over five feet six inches in height, his build compact rather than slight, and suggested adequate strength instead of power. Like so many young men who have survived the bitter fighting of the war just ended, he looked older than his actual years, which totaled twenty-eight. He had a long face with regular features that gave him a nondescript handsomeness. His mouthline was gentle, his nose straight, and his coal black eyes honest. His hair was prematurely gray with only a few hanks of dark red to show its former coloration. It was trimmed neat and short, and this was the only obvious sign of the five years he had spent in the army of the Confederate States.

The city was very quiet as Steele entered the streets of its southern section and he was mildly surprised at this. Washington was the capital of the victorious northern states and he had expected it still to be in the throes of triumphant revelry even this long after Lee's surrender. But he did not give too much thought to the matter, for he had another, more important subject on his mind. He had no trouble finding his way to his destination, for he had been a frequent visitor to the city in pre-war days and little had changed during the intervening years.

It was not until he turned onto Tenth Street that he pulled up short in surprise. The street was as quiet as all the others had been, but there was a difference. Where the others had been deserted, this one was crowded with people. The great majority of them were huddled together in a large group before a house diagonally across the street from the darkened façade of Ford's Theatre. Occasionally, one or more of the silent spectators would drift away from the crowd. One such was an old woman who stepped unwittingly in front of Steele's horse as he urged the animal forward. She looked at the rider, showing no emotion at almost being trampled. Deep shock dwelled behind her moist eyes.

"What's happening here, ma'am?" Steele asked, his voice smoothed by a Virginia drawl as he touched his hat brim with a gloved hand.

The old woman blinked, and a tear was squeezed from the corner of each eye. "Mr. Lincoln," she replied tremulously. "They've shot Mr. Lincoln."

Under different circumstances, Steele knew he might have felt a surge of joy and expectation that the event could signal new hope for the South to rise against defeat. But he had come to Washington determined to forget the past and adjust himself to the best future he could make. Even so, he had difficulty in injecting a degree of the mournful into his voice as he asked, "Is the President dead?"

The old woman shook her head. "He's dying. Won't last out the night, they say."

Steele took a final look down the street, then jerked over the reins to angle his horse toward Elmer's Barroom. It was not in complete darkness, for a dim light flickered far back in one of the windows. After he had looped the reins over the hitching rail at the edge of the sidewalk, he approached the doors and they swung open in front of him.

"We're closed, mister," Elmer announced as the newcomer crossed the threshold. "Mark of respect for the President."

The doors squeaked closed behind Steele and he halted abruptly. He saw Elmer standing behind the bar, using the turned-down light of a single kerosene lamp to count the night's takings. "I just heard," he said, moving toward the bar. "After getting news like that, a man needs a drink. Whiskey."

He pulled up short again as something brushed against his shoulder. As he looked up, he could see the limply hanging form of a dead man. The body revolved slowly from where he had collided with a dangling leg. "Turn up the lamp, bartender," he said softly.

Elmer continued to chink loose change, taking it from his apron pocket and stacking it on the bartop. "Told you, mister, the place is closed up for the night," he growled.

"You don't turn up that lamp, I'll kill you," Steele said, his drawling voice still pitched low. But it was high on menace.

Elmer's head snapped up and he peered intently through the darkness toward the newcomer. He could not see Steele clearly and it was for this reason he reached out and turned up the wick. His free hand dragged a Manhattan Navy Model out from beneath the bar. When the pool of light had spread far enough to illuminate Steele and the hanging man, the revolver was cocked and aimed. "You don't look capable, mister," Elmer said, noting that Steele wore no gunbelt and his hands were empty.

Steele was staring up at the swollen face of the old man. His own features were empty of expression and when he turned to look at Elmer and started to walk toward him he still gave no outward sign of what he was thinking. "What happened here?" he asked, the threat missing from his low tones. But neither was he concerned with the pointing gun in the bartender's hands. He glanced casually to his right and saw a bearded old timer with a bloody forehead climbing painfully to his feet. Then to the left, where a sleeping drunk was just a lumpy shadow against a deeper shadow beneath the table.

Elmer's sullen eyes met Steele's open stare, then took in at close range the man's easy-going features and unprovoking build. He lumped all this together with the lack of visible weapons and decided his unwanted customer had a tough mouth but nothing with which to back it up. He put the gun down beneath the bar and started to dig for more coins. "A guy blasted the President over at the theatre," he rasped. "Got clean away." He nodded toward the man hanging from the beam. "That guy passed the gun to the murderer. Didn't have the sense to take it on the lam." A sour grin twisted his mouth. "Me and a few others kinda forced him to hang around."

The old timer was leaning his elbows on the bar, nursing his broken head in the palms of his hands. "Weren't no proof of that!" he snapped, without looking up. "Ed Binns and his pals just up and hanged the old man on account of what you told 'em."

Elmer glowered hatefully at the old timer. "He give the gun to Booth, I'm telling you," he snarled.

"And you can give me a drink," Steele said.

Elmer sighed, seemed about to refuse, then swung around and swept a shot glass and bottle from the shelf behind him. He set the glass on the bartop and poured the right measure without looking.

Steele proffered no money, and neither did he reach for the drink. "What if you were wrong?" he asked.

Elmer banged the bottle down angrily. "Just drink your drink and get out so I can close up," he ordered. "I weren't wrong."

151

"You were wrong," Steele said. With his left hand, Steele tugged at his ear lobe. His right hand came fast out of the pocket on that side of the jacket and Elmer's eyes widened with terror as he saw the tiny two-shot derringer clutched in the fist. The gun went off with a small crack. The shattered whiskey bottle made a louder noise. Elmer fell backward, crashing against the display shelf. His hands clutched at his bulbous stomach. Small shards of broken glass glittered against the dark stains of whiskey covering his apron. He looked down at himself and gasped when he saw the blood oozing between his fingers.

"His name was Benjamin Steele. And my name is Adam Steele," the man said softly. "That was my father you killed."

The pain had had time to reach Elmer now, and it overflowed his eyes in the form of tears as he brought his head up to look at the man he had so badly misjudged. Steele held the shocked stare of the other, as he slid the derringer back into his pocket and used his left hand to draw out a match. He struck it on his thumbnail and in the sudden flare of yellow light his eyes seemed not to be as one with the rest of his features. For the lines of his face had a composed, innocuous set—while the eyes, pulled wide, blazed with a seemingly unquenchable fury.

Then the flaring match was arced forward. Elmer emitted a strangled sob of horror, throwing up his hands. The match sailed between them and bounced against his chest. It fell to the floor, but not before a fragile flame licked up from the whiskey-sodden material of his shirt. He beat at it with a blood-stained hand, the motion fanning the fire. Within a terrifying few seconds, as the fury died within Steele, the bartender's massive body was enveloped in searing flames. As shreds of charred clothing fell from him and the intense heat swept over his naked skin, his sobs became strangled cries. He threw himself to the floor and began to roll backward and forward as he beat at the hungry flames. But the whiskey-soaked sawdust only added fuel to the agonizing fire.

The old timer's horror at the lynching was nothing compared to the revulsion he felt as he watched Elmer's pitifully ineffectual attempts to beat out the flames. But he made no effort to intervene, conscious of the evil lurking beneath the deceptively gentle surface of the young man standing beside him.

"Innocent man getting lynched," Steele said, still softly. "Fair burns a man up, doesn't it?"

* * *

The hole was almost as deep as Adam Steele was tall. Reverently he lowered the stiff body of the old man into the bare earth, not looking down into the trench until the corpse was completely covered. Then he worked furiously to shovel the rest of the dirt onto the grave. His fury grew as he realized he wouldn't be able to place a marker on the site.

He gazed once again at the still-smoking ruins of the Steele home. Only a few items were worth salvaging. Souvenirs of better, peaceful days. But Adam would only take one reminder. An unusual weapon, a Colt Hartford sporting rifle, six-shot revolving percussion, .44 caliber, given to his father by the President. The barrel was covered with soot, and the rosewood stock was slightly charred, but the action worked smoothly.

Now Lincoln and Ben Steele were both dead. Two fine lives extinguished by madness . . . two burials marked the beginning of an unending and blood-soaked vengeance trail for Adam Steele.

EDGE

→ BY ←
George G. Gilman

Josiah Hedges is no ordinary man — he's a violent gunslinger. Created out of fury, hardened by death and destruction, he's rough, but not as rough as the fate of those who get in his way.

Over 3.5 million copies sold!